RP

RADDELL PUBLISHING

CATCH ME

CATCH ME

TIMOTHY RADDELL

Raddell Publishing

Raddell Publishing, LLC.

ISBN 978-1-962105-00-2

Ebook ISBN 978-1-962105-01-9

raddellpublishing.com

Faustina Maria Raddell

ORA PRO NOBIS

1

The shooter's footsteps come right up to the doorway. The sharp clink of a rifle's bolt echoes in the empty hall. Behind the door, someone lets out a breath. Everyone in the classroom shoots inaudible curses at the unfortunate student. Even the teacher's eyes hurl a desperate and hateful accusation. But JP barely notices what his classmates are doing behind him, to some poor soul who dares to breathe while they all cower in the corner. JP's eyes focus on the door handle in front of him. A chair floats above his head, ready to be brought down, ready to kill, so that the others who don't have the courage to fight for themselves might be spared. Something shifts on the other side. They are both ready. JP and the other. The handle wobbles and begins to turn.

"Mr. Sheen?"

John Philip Sheen tore his eyes from his daydream to look up at sharp-nosed Mrs. Scheider bearing down at him from the front of the class. "Yes?"

"Can you answer the question?"

JP rubbed his chin, acting like he had to ponder before he replied, "Can't say that I can."

The teacher raised her eyebrows, pretending to be surprised.

"How about you just repeat it for the class?"

"Sure. You asked me, 'can you answer the question?'" JP said smugly.

Several people laughed. Mrs. Scheider's lips twisted into an unpleasant smile. "You're right, Mr. Sheen. I should give you a gold star, shouldn't I? Such a clever answer, you really should be proud of yourself. If only you applied your wit to the rest of your schoolwork you wouldn't have an F. You'd be surprised what you might accomplish."

The kid next to JP breathed out sharply. No one said anything or laughed, but JP imagined they were all going crazy in their heads. Someone would be bound to offer him some aloe after a public burn like that.

Mrs. Scheider turned back to the blackboard with a knowingly triumphant grin. She didn't even bother to ask the original question again, whatever it had been. But everyone's eyes were now on JP sitting in the back row. Most of them had been disturbed out of their own daydreams to be witness to his humiliation. JP met every glance till they turned away, ashamed to have been caught staring.

Once his classmates were put back in their place, JP turned his attention to the front. And no, not to learn anything about chemical bonds, but to mentally hurl slurs at his teacher. He laughed in his throat when he called her a snaggle-toothed hag, which drew another few glances. But most of his classmates were too far away in their own Neverlands to even wipe the drool from their lips, let alone turn their heads around to look at him again.

A yawn escaped from JP and soon traveled up and down the rows of desks. Mrs. Scheider simply increased the volume of her lecture and illustrated four carbon atoms bonding on the blackboard. Didn't she understand that the football team won last night? Didn't she understand that they were all up till dawn drinking? Anyone who wasn't a loser, anyway. Not that JP would have been sober if they lost. Or if they had not played at all, for that matter. But the fact was, none of them were listening. Even if they weren't all tired and hungover, they still wouldn't care about chemical bonds.

One kid in the far corner of the room was so out of it that he was trying to follow along with the lesson while looking at his textbook upside down. The kid next to him had his face covered in ink markings. He had been poking himself with his pen for the last half an hour in order to stay awake. JP's buddy Cortez had his eyes open, but there was no responsiveness in them. After three full years of three varsity sports on top of late-night parties, he had developed the ability to appear awake while he slept. JP and many of their classmates admired the skill and the man.

Most kids JP knew, or at least the ones he talked to, didn't care about any of their classes. He slept through most of them himself, except Gym, and that was not from lack of trying. Fat Phyllis, the gym teacher, had on several occasions condemned him to running for the duration of class after finding him curled up between the volleyball nets. JP smiled at a memory of Fat Phyllis, despite his hatred for her—in fact, because of that hatred for her.

JP had many fond memories of the teachers he hated. These memories consisted of cars covered in honey, defaced chalkboards, and unveiled personal lives. They were the small and numerous acts of revenge he had taken on teachers who had wronged him. JP had no such memories with Mrs. Scheider, but he had a feeling one might be in the making.

JP rubbed his eyes and then looked at his twitching fingers. He put his pen between his index and middle finger and held it in his mouth. It would keep him still for now, but damn, he wanted a cigarette. The fingers on his other hand began to tap the imitation wood of his desk, and the brunette, Kathrine, who sat two seats from him, looked over and smiled. It was a knowing smile, coy and playful. She bit her lip, messing up her red lipstick. Now, maybe JP was very tired, but it looked like her eyelashes fluttered like a dove. It was too much, in his opinion. It made her look like she was having an epileptic episode. Didn't she know he had a girlfriend already?

"Uh-oh," he thought, remembering the morning.

Please don't say I did it again.

Red lipstick. He should have known. Madison never wore red. Well, now he knew whom the lipstick had belonged to. But he still wondered why he found it on his—maybe it would be best not to mention where.

Well, Madison had yet to find out about any of the other times, so as long as Hot Lips over there kept her lips closed from now on, so would he. But judging by the fluttering of her eyes, that might be too much to hope for.

Happy thoughts, JP. Happy thoughts.

Like what he was going to do tonight. The same thing as every night: get drunk with his friends, smoke a few cigarettes, maybe spend the night at Madison's. He was the Pinky and the

Brain of alcoholic teenagers. Unfortunately, much like the real Pinky and the Brain, his plans often went awry, and he woke up in strange beds. Or even, at times, beds that were sadly, not strange enough.

But these were supposed to be happy thoughts. And they were!

Besides the odd screwup that didn't hurt anyone anyways, his only real regret about his nightly routine was that it only happened at night. JP was not sure how he could get through school without his nightly excitement to look forward to. He was sure learning about chemical bonds would kill him without $C_8H_{11}NO_2$ and CH_3CH_2OH. Or as normal people know them, dopamine and alcohol.

A loud noise approaches from outside. Like a drumroll, the air beats against the earth in a rhythm. Everyone gets up from their chairs and looks out the window. But JP knows what it is—a helicopter. He knows who is in it and what they want. And he knows they'll kill anyone who gets in their way.

The bell rang, and JP was ripped from yet another fantasy. *"And that was going to be a good one, "*he thought mournfully. Though, to be honest, JP hadn't decided if they were the Feds or the Russians. Russians were a solid choice for any villain, but right then, he felt the weight of an overreaching authority in the form of Mrs. Scheider, so he decided it ought to be the Feds. It didn't matter, class was over. Everyone filed out, and JP tried to fall in line but was stopped with a "Mr. Sheen!"

JP cringed at the sound of his last name. What now?

He walked over to Mrs. Scheider's desk. "Yes?"

"Would you like an opportunity for extra credit?" she asked. Before a 'no' could pass JP's tongue, Mrs. Scheider cut him off. "On second thought, don't bother answering. The answer is, you need it. And there is an opportunity tonight at the city library. Go to the presentation at seven and you might not fail."

"Okay," he said, a very defeated okay. What else could he say?

Mrs. Scheider smiled. "Good."

JP would rather get killed by Russians than have to listen to a lecture after school. But she was right, he needed the extra credit. His parents would kill him if he flunked, and they were not as kind as the Russians.

"What's the lecture on?" JP asked, hoping for something interesting like *the chemistry of explosives*.

"Free Will and Neuroscience."

JP groaned.

"You might like it. It's a rather important topic in science and philosophy." She made it sound like important topics in science and philosophy ought to be interesting to teenagers who would rather be doing anything else.

"At least tell me that I get a gold star for attending."

Mrs. Scheider smiled. "Only if you manage to stay awake the whole time, and no zoning out either."

JP groaned again. He was not going to get that gold star.

Dejected, JP left the classroom. Traffic in the hall was sparse. The third floor was always empty. Only a few people had lockers here. JP was one of them. He appreciated the solitude. The second and first floors were far too crowded. But after getting his backpack from his locker, he braved his way to the first floor to tell Madison he could not do anything tonight.

"Hey, JP, can I get you some aloe? Looks like you got a nasty burn in chemistry today," a kid named Steph yelled to him as he walked down the stairs.

"No, I'm good. I hear your mom likes men with scars."

"Great comeback!" Steph said. "Real clever. You should get a gold star for that one."

"Dammit, it is not my day!" JP exclaimed.

Absorbed in thought and in catching pencils, books, and loose papers as they fell from her locker, Madison did not notice him approach. She had dark brown hair, green eyes, and an awkward but truly genuine smile always on her face.

After a long moment of watching her, JP said, "Here's to looking at you, kid."

She gave a little jump but then smiled at him.

"What were you thinking of?" he asked.

She bit her top lip and looked off into the depths of her locker. "Do you ever just stay up all night, thinking about things?"

"Almost every night."

"Really?" She turned to him.

"Absolutely," he said, looking down the hall. "Like, what are things anyway? Are there things that are the same as other things or are all things different? Or maybe all things are the same. They say it's all reducible to energy, so is what we perceive as things really just collections of tiny particles of one universal thing? Ockham said there were no Universals, but can we say that when we look at two like atoms, if there are absolutely no differences—"

She punched him in the shoulder, and he stopped with a smug grin.

"Oh, come on. I have a whole theory."

"I'm sure you do. But I was being serious."

"So was I."

Madison pursed her lips. She handed him her pink soccer

bag, to hold while she gathered the rest of her books. Her thoughts returned to wherever they had been before JP disrupted her.

"So, I have some bad news," JP said. "I've gotten roped into going to a lecture tonight for extra credit. Which means I can't do anything later."

To JP's surprise, she let out a sigh of relief.

"What was that?" he asked.

"It's nothing, I just have something to do after practice. So, I'm glad you have something too."

He stuck his tongue out. "You may be glad, but you're not the one who has to go to a lecture on Free Will and Neuroscience."

"You'll enjoy that, Mr. What Are Things Anyway."

"Maybe if it didn't cut into my own time. I've got nothing to look forward to now. Might as well just stay at school."

"How about you come to my practice?" Madison suggested. She made her eyes big and gave him one of her signature awkward smiles. With an exaggerated sigh, he said yes. She gave a little hop and then hugged him. "You're the best!"

"I know."

Madison zipped up her bookbag and closed her locker.

"I'll have to stop at home first, but we can walk out together," JP said.

"Actually, I've got to print something off at the library. Why don't you go ahead."

"Okay, I'll see you at the field."

"Thanks," she said and left him with a kiss on the cheek and that smile.

As soon as JP closed his car door, he reached into his book bag. It didn't take long for him to pull out the pack of cigarettes. It was the only thing he kept in the bag. It was nestled beside the bottle of Jack his buddy Kyle had scored for him, but that would soon be hidden away under his bed. He didn't need to take any books home because any homework he did do, was completed in his first period study hall. He lit the cigarette and tossed the lighter in his cupholder. After a relieving drag, he turned on the car and started home.

Despite the pleasure of the cigarette, JP's nostrils were flaring.

Dammit, Mrs. Scheider. Stupid lecture. Stupid school. It's not like anyone learns anything in high school. They make a big fuss about it and try to make everyone miserable, and then they force everyone to go to a university after.

At least there would be bigger parties in college. But he'd still get belittled by professors who think they are all-knowing, though they have no connection to reality.

JP got so wrapped up in how much he hated school that he forgot to ash his cigarette. Instead, the smoldering ash dropped on his favorite Adidas joggers. With a yelp and a quick swipe of his hand, he brushed it away. He looked up just in time to slam on the brakes since the car in front of him had stopped at a light.

Flustered, JP tossed the unfinished butt out the window. Stupid school. Stupid ash. Stupid people in front of him driving slow. He was so frustrated that he forgot to cover up the smell of cigarettes with an air freshener.

When JP walked into his home, he was halted by the sight of his mother standing by the kitchen table, waiting. Waiting for him. Her back was tense and rigid, as if instead of a spine, brittle iron rods supported her shoulders. With gray hair that got grayer by the minute, she looked less like a person and more like a steel cage.

"John Philip Sheen, what were these doing under your bed!" She indicated the two half-full bottles of whiskey and a particularly nice bottle of authentic Mexican tequila. It always stood out to him because it had a glass handle molded into it. He'd never seen a bottle like it. Usually, tequila bottles were clear, but this bottle was brown with a blue label.

At the sight of his hidden treasures exposed, JP tightened his grip on the straps of his backpack. His mother advanced but was halted by her nose. "And why do you smell like cigarettes?"

Nothing came forth from the overwhelmed JP, so she badgered him with accusations. When JP's silence continued, the cage broke, and his mother's reprimands turned into shouting.

"Shit," JP whispered under his breath. Unfortunately, he did not whisper well enough.

"What did you say? Don't think you're too old to be spanked, Mister!" She brandished a wooden spoon, still dripping from the simmering soup on the stove.

"What will I find next?" his mother exclaimed, sorrow mixing with the anger. "You'll come home tomorrow and tell me you got a girl pregnant. Or worse, you won't tell me, and you won't care about that poor girl or the baby."

This imaginary scenario she thought up made her angrier, as if she decided he had already done it.

"What else are you hiding around your room?"

"Nothing."

"So, if I search your car, I won't find any hidden stash of drugs."

"No, and I don't do drugs, Mom."

"Tobacco and alcohol are drugs!"

He threw up his arms in a gesture that meant, "*What does it matter?*"

"What about those cigarettes? You obviously just smoked

one! Hand them over, Mister."

"Fine." JP reached into his bag, rustled around for the open pack, and prayed his mother did not sneak a peek and see the Jack and the rest of the cigarettes. He saw her leaning over to get a better look. He found and then flung the half-emptied pack onto the ground at her feet. She glared at it, angry at the fact that he had cigarettes, but angrier at the way he tossed it to her. Quickly, JP zipped up his bag. She started to scream again.

More accusations. And then a rampage of promises. Promises like being grounded for life, getting his phone taken away, and anything else she could imagine would hurt him. At least she hadn't found his search history. She ended the berating with, "Just wait until your father wakes up from his nap!"

Tact forgotten in all the yelling that still rang in his ears, JP said, "I'm sure he's already awake after hearing you shout for the last ten minutes."

This prompted more shouting. JP weighed his options. He could lie, but that would fail. She knew too much already. He could remain silent and hope for the best, but that would mean grounding for life as a minimum. Or he could defend his position, explain his independence, tell her that his decisions were his own and he would bear the consequences if they came. However, he wasn't sure he was ready to bear the consequences of that particular statement, since he lived in her house.

"What else will you pull out of that bag!" It was a statement, not a question. JP supposed she imagined that a decapitated head might be in there, or something worse. But he was not going to wait around for that statement to turn into a real question. He turned around and exited the way he came. "Don't you walk away from me, Mister! You get back here right now."

Well, since his mother was already sure to kill him, there was no need to go to the lecture at the library tonight. But this small solace did nothing to quell the anger growing in JP's mind. What right did she have to yell at him? He wasn't her property. He was his own self. JP longed to be free of it, his mother, school, heck, even the guilt he felt about Madison. What did he owe any of them? Well, at least Madison didn't try to control him. The guilt came as a consequence of their relationship. And his carelessness.

Madison's soccer practice was at the park, conveniently located a few blocks down. He always enjoyed having a smoke and watching some girl-on-girl action in a contact sport. His bag was still on his shoulder, and he decided to walk, not drive. Maybe he could get his buddy Kyle to join him. Kyle was dating Regan, Madison's best friend, who was also on the team, and JP desperately needed someone to vent to. But JP got the sense that Kyle would try to give him some advice, like to go home. To apologize, which JP didn't want to hear.

Cars roared past him, neighbors shouted hello, dogs barked, and JP heard none of it. Thoughts of despair and anger shouted in his head. There were so many thoughts that he could not distinguish between them. His mind became one muddled mess of frustration. He walked straight into the park, ignoring the sidewalks, trampling on the freshly mown grass.

A hill overlooked the soccer field. There were a few trees that shaded it from the sun, and it commanded a complete view of the park. He trudged up its grassy slope from the rear and sat at the top. The girls' soccer team was still putting on their cleats and stretching out. Madison was setting out cones for some drills. She noticed him and waved.

Damn, her in those shorts was an especially welcome sight right now. He pulled out a fresh pack of cigarettes from his bag and then reached into his pocket. A curse followed. His lighter sat in the cupholder of his car.

His fingers twitched. They were begging him, prostrate in supplication. He relented with a miserable whimper and stood up. He walked back over the hill. In his impatience, his foot caught a stone, and he stumbled down the slope. He made it to the bottom still on his feet, but the air was rushing past his ears. He was going too fast. There was a line of bushes in front of him that promised to scrape and scratch. Rather than hurtle into the foliage, he chose to fall on the grass. Tumbling down, he rolled to a stop, nose sniffing the fresh-cut blades of the lawn. A whiny curse blew into the ground.

"You okay, kid?" asked a passing jogger. "Need some help?"

JP looked up at the man. "Yeah, just a minute." He pressed his nose back into the grass to mope a bit longer. A shadow passed over JP, and he figured it was the jogger standing in the way of the sun. But when JP looked up, the jogger was gone, and a stray cloud had caused the shadow.

What kind of person offers someone help and then bolts away? Even more frustrated than before, JP walked back to his house. And again, he heard nothing, no roaring of cars, no neighbors' hellos, no barks, nor anything else.

There was a chance his parents might spot him going into his car and come out yelling. That, he could not risk. Any confrontation in his current state would surely lead to further escalation. And at the moment, he was not prepared to get kicked out of the house. So, he snuck up to the window to see where they were.

He could not spot them and tried another window. There was no sign there, either. Maybe they were upstairs. But through the kitchen window, JP could see the soup boiling over, something his stiff-backed mother would never allow, not even when she was overboiled enough herself to wake his father from a post-work nap. Their cars were still in the drive, so they had not left. Then, something glittered in the corner of his eye. Two of his bottles of alcohol still stood on the kitchen table. Seemed a shame, to let his mother pour them down the drain. Immediate action was called for.

Breath held, JP opened the door and listened. No sound but the bubbling of the soup. He slunk over to the oven. Turning off the flame, he paused to listen again. Shouldn't they be talking? Steaming? Fuming! Crying! Or really, anything up there? He could usually hear if a conversation was taking place upstairs, but there was only silence.

Here he was, being miserable, expecting the worst, and they didn't even care about it. They had finally given up. Did this mean they wouldn't punish him? Doubtful. But this did mean that home would be that much more boring.

He looked up the shag-carpeted stairs. He couldn't resist. He had to know what they were doing. Step by careful step, he climbed. Long practice of sneaking home late at night had taught him every creak to avoid. At the fifth step, he halted and raised his ear. Where were they? He half expected them to come streaking through the front door and catch him lurking on the stairs like a thief.

At the top, he peeked into the first room. This one was his own room, but that had obviously not prevented his mother from entering and finding the stash beneath his bed. The spare bedroom was equally as empty. The bathroom door was open, and they weren't there, which left his parents' room. He tried to put himself at an angle and peep in slowly. But when at last he surveyed the entire room, they were absent.

It had only been twenty minutes. JP checked his phone, hoping for a message, no matter how angry it might be. But they had not texted him. In fact, no one had called, texted, or Snapped him. Unusual. His phone was normally blowing up with messages. And Madison at least ought to have asked why he left the field.

His first instinct was to text her. Delivered, not read. Minutes passed with no response.

But that makes sense. Right? She is doing soccer drills and can't check her phone.

That did not stop him from pacing the kitchen. The empty house felt wrong. The entire day felt wrong. He could not make sense of it. Where did they go?

The two bottles on the table were begging him to take them and run. But where was his tequila? That's the one he really wanted.

His brittle mother and his tired father did not show up. But the tequila did make an appearance. It was uncorked, tilted, and abandoned in the sink.

Empty.

Wasted.

JP wished his parents would never come home. This was his special treat, the one thing he was willing to wait for. He'd already had it for two years and had been waiting till he actually turned twenty-one to drink it. He had that day all planned out. It would start at noon with the opening of this bottle, and then he and Madison would—

But Madison had still not answered, and no one else had texted him. After all that had happened today already, JP expected the worst. Maybe she got knocked in the head going after the soccer ball. He texted Regan, her best friend, but it was the same with her. He scrolled through his contact list, texting everyone on the team, until he came to the name Kathrine.

"Hot Lips!"

Maybe she told Madison. JP wasn't even sure that he had done anything with Hot Lips. Then again, he couldn't be sure he *didn't* do anything, either. There was a distinct portion of last night that he could not remember. But that would explain why none of the girls were responding. They had done the same thing to Terry Anderson. He hadn't realized why his now-ex-girlfriend and every other girl in school ignored him for an entire month. JP had been the one to break it to him. And it turned out that he hadn't even done it.

Kyle would know or could find out. JP texted him, but after several minutes, no one had replied. Maybe Regan had ordered him not to talk to JP either. Next, he called a different Bro but got his voicemail. JP started chewing on his collar because he had run out of fingernails to bite off.

Maybe all this was in his head. He was just panicking because of being caught earlier. Or maybe he had smacked his head harder than he realized when he hit the ground at the bottom of the hill. There was only one way JP could be sure. He ran outside and hopped in his car.

There were no other vehicles on the road, so JP pushed upwards of sixty in a thirty-five. Turning onto another street, he nearly crashed into two cars idled in the middle of the road. Both lanes were completely blocked. He gave up honking when neither moved and got out of his car. Red-faced, he walked up between them, explosive words on his lips. But both cars were empty, abandoned, engines still on.

Is there a killer on the loose and everyone but me got the memo to hide?

He ran to the nearest house and started banging on the door.

"Hello? Somebody! Is anybody there?" No one came. Then the next house and the next. Eventually, he gave up and ran the rest of the way to the park. He came from the back way and climbed the hill again. He got to the top, looked around, and collapsed to his knees. Soccer balls littered the field. Cars were in the parking lot. Sports bags filled the sidelines. But there was not a living soul around. Only a squirrel, which occupied itself by digging in one of the bags.

JP lay there, quiet in this silent world.

Everyone was gone.

He noticed the wind first, how it caressed the leaves of the trees. Then the bird song. Even the prick of the grass became sharper under his hands. The world was still here. But the part of it that he cared about had vanished. The wind grew louder and colder. He shivered. The part of the world that had Madison in it was gone.

It's not possible. People don't disappear into thin air. Well, maybe they do.

That would explain the jogger. He had walked all the way home without noticing the emptiness. All the way home, concerned with only his own problems.

JP looked up toward the sun, and for the first time, he noticed how lonely it must be up in the blue sky. At least the moon had the stars all around it.

Well, maybe there was somebody else. Some glittering star. If he were still here, why not someone else? But whom? And where?

At least he wouldn't have to deal with his parents' reprimands anymore. Nor would he have to wake up and go to school, to sit through dull lectures on chemical bonds, or the neuroscience of free will. In fact, he wouldn't have to deal with anyone's crap.

He sat up, encouraged by this line of thought. It was not just what he would not have to do anymore, he could now do anything he wanted.

He'd never have to face the consequences of Hot Lips or any of the others. Madison would never find out now. He fell back to the grass. This thought sucked worse than any other that day. He could not allow it to linger.

He had freedom, true freedom to do what he wanted, to be who he wanted. He could not waste it moping. What he wanted to use this freedom for most of all, were two things. He wanted to get another bottle of that special tequila, which would probably take a while. But the more urgent desire was to get drunk and burn down the school.

Who would care anyway? The squirrel? JP walked down the hill toward the cluster of soccer bags. The squirrel had hopped away with a white plastic object sticking out of his mouth. As JP drew closer, the fuzzball twitched its tail, dropped the object, and bolted up a tree. It was a pregnancy test, unwrapped and used. If he remembered how it worked, then this one read positive.

Lucky girl dodged a life of servitude.

He'd take disappearing into nothingness any day over the

slavery of dirty diapers.

Madison's pink bag lay open, her cleats still inside, along with her shin guards. But JP was only interested in her keys, which were in the side pocket. Yet he took the whole bag. He got in her white SUV and went down to the gas station to get his needed supplies: gasoline, beer, and cigarettes.

When he arrived, he spotted something strange at one of the pumps. Or rather, something normal. A man, tall and bald, was filling his car at the pump. JP's jaw dropped a little and then morphed into a grin. He was not alone after all.

"Hey." He walked over to the man. "Do you have any idea what's happened?"

The man looked a little shocked at hearing JP. Maybe he had thought he was the only one left. Recovering within a second, the man said, "Everyone's disappeared, that's what's happened."

"I gathered that. I mean, do you know why?"

"Aliens, the Russians, the Rapture, take your pick." The man clearly thought it was a stupid question.

JP put on a thoughtful expression. "Definitely aliens."

The car was a hoarder's nest, filled to the brim with blankets, boxes, and cases of water. On top were tied several propane tanks and an inflatable water doughnut that seemed to be filled with some sort of liquid.

Confused and a little uncomfortable, JP asked, "Whatcha

doing?”

“Preparing.”

“For what? If you’re talking about preparing for the Apocalypse, then you’re a little late, aren’t you?”

“Look, kid, I still got to eat, to drink, be warm, be safe. I’m getting everything I need to live.”

“Same,” JP said, though his necessities looked a little different from the bald man’s, and they did not include a water doughnut.

“Well, good luck, kid.”

“You too.”

When the man had gone, JP jumped in the air. The melancholy that underwrote his new freedom was dissipating. He wondered if anyone he knew still remained, or if everyone he met would be new to him. He’d miss some people, certainly, but the cure for that was in the cooler right before him.

Now, Coors or Miller? He stroked his chin thoughtfully.

“Oh well,” he said as if the question were hopeless. “Better take both.”

Despite how long JP searched, he could not find gas cans at the gas station. The man with the water doughnut on his car had probably taken them, if there were any. JP ran across the street to a convenience store and disappeared for twenty minutes. When he came out again, a bag full of snacks hung from his left hand, but he had been unable to find anything like a gas can. It dawned on him that the man might have faced a similar problem. In his other hand was a child-sized inflatable pool doughnut, with a green dinosaur head sticking out from one side.

The part air would normally be blown into was too small to insert the nozzle of the pump directly. He had to devise a funnel of some sort, or else spill half the gas onto the concrete. Not that he would mind wasting the gas, but he didn't like the idea of covering the ground he stood on with a flammable substance.

This whole thing was becoming tedious, and he wanted to get the school well on fire before sunset, so he had to hurry. After thinking about the problem a little longer, he burst into a run back over to the convenience store. In full stride, JP came out with a large plastic bin raised over his head. The bin set at the base of the pump, he ran into the station and turned on the gas. He filled the bin up and then submerged his dinosaur in the gas till it was bursting. Closing the cap, he lifted it out. He dumped some water on it to get rid of any excess gasoline and then gingerly placed it in the back of Madison's car.

Yes, it was a disaster waiting to happen, but JP figured that enough bad stuff had happened to him today, so the odds were in his favor.

There were still a lot of cars parked at the high school. Cars he recognized. They belonged to the kids he had struggled through school with, for the past four years. He would do this for them. One last tribute for the ones he would miss.

He walked down the main hall, a twenty-four pack in one hand, the Dino doughnut in the other, and cigarettes packing his pockets. There was a glass case outside the principal's office. It contained all the trophies and awards collectively won by the students over the years. This was the first thing to go. The bronze bust of Augustine of Hippo, which sat on the principal's desk, caught JP's attention. Taking it, he posed outside the glass case like a baseball player. After sternly looking to his left and right in mock fashion, he pitched it into the trophies. Shards exploded everywhere.

The rest of the school got the same treatment. He hooked up his phone to the PA system and blasted Pop Punk and other 2000s Rock as he tossed chairs out of windows, desks down stairwells, and computers into toilets. All the while, there was a beer in one hand and a cigarette hanging from his mouth. After throwing things lost its splendor, he started drawing. No surface remained free of defacement. When drawing dicks was no longer flavorful, he started writing racial slurs on the lockers of black students and then equally racist responses on those of white kids. This morphed into a whole racially charged conversation between lockers.

Most of these slurs and jokes, JP hadn't even made up. He

was reusing other people's material. Some of the jokes he scribbled on the lockers were originally said by the kids the lockers belonged to. It didn't matter to him. No one would know or care. Not that they cared when they were still there. Everyone in his high school was somehow both very racist and not racist at all. A paradox everyone lived with and never questioned.

It ended with the black lockers winning decisively. And thus, the white lockers' mother would ever remain a snaggle-toothed ho. This was simple honesty on JP's part. He knew that any war of insults would be dominated by just a few people, of which the most savage was his buddy Cortez, who was black.

JP did not touch Mrs. Scheider's room. He figured that it should burn as-is. After mocking him for failing in front of the entire class and then forcing him into attending that lecture that only fortune spared him from, Mrs. Scheider held a special place in his hate. One that required no preamble, one that deserved only flames. He did, however, riffle through her desk until he came away with a whole roll of gold-star stickers. He placed one on his shirt and said to an imagined Mrs. Scheider, "You know, you were right, Old Sharp Nose!" His voice slurred from the alcohol, he added, "I have accomplished quite a lot, now that I finally applied myself to this school."

There is no need to describe what JP did inside the principal's office, other than that he used a picture of the principal's wife to do it. Nothing about the school was sacred to him. Around thirteen beers and twenty cigarettes in, he, in his inebriated state, thought it was a job well done. Somehow, he made his way to the library. He toppled a few bookshelves, popped the dinosaur, and flicked a half-finished cigarette over his shoulder onto the books. It was cool. He knew it. It was made doubly so from all the alcohol polluting his blood.

He left the building, sat on Madison's car, and cracked open another beer. He watched it burn as the night rose. And in the darkness, he saw that other fires were blazing in the distance. Had someone else lit them? Or maybe they were accidental and now there was no one to stop them.

"Wow," he said. It was strange. And the strangeness made it exciting. But how did it happen, this whole situation? If it was aliens, then how? And why? His mind swam in the alcohol, trying to make sense of why most people had simply vanished.

Maybe the aliens had teleported everyone up to their ships and were doing experiments? JP imagined Mrs. Scheider getting probed by an alien and cheersed the flaming school at the thought. But the more he thought, the more he realized that he could do nothing to discover the reason everyone disappeared. The only way he would know is if the reason revealed itself to him. Which was unlikely to happen.

JP laughed to himself. Such strange realizations came to

him when he was drunk. Thoughts he would have spent days and weeks coming to terms with if he were sober, became simple with a little alcohol. Simple. That is how he liked things. Perhaps that's why he was able to deal with everyone being gone, because it made everything simple.

The wind blew loudly, and the fire crackled and burst, hungry dogs howled, locked in their houses, but there were no cars, no sirens, no people yelling at him for burning down the school.

This was going to be fun.

2

Waking up the next morning was not fun. Somehow, he had driven home and woken up in his own bed. Thanks to his well-maintained tolerance for alcohol, the hangover only consisted of a throbbing head and a slight stomachache. Naturally, he stayed in bed for a few hours, though he was not sure for how long. His digital clock had stopped working. He sat up, regretted it, lay down, got up again, and made his way to the shower. Eyes barely open, he let the water run for a moment to warm up. He jumped in and then leapt out. The water was freezing and wouldn't warm up. And the longer it ran, the weaker it got, till it was but a trickle.

It took JP several minutes to realize the power was out. When it finally clicked, he recalled the man at the gas station. He had to get what he would need to survive, i.e.: a warm shower. But where to find a place with water and power if the whole city was down, as he supposed it was? If he wanted water, he remembered that his uncle's place in the country had its own well. Although the sulfur smell of well water would take some getting used to. So, all he needed to do was find a country house with a generator or something.

Madison's car was parked on his lawn. By some miracle, he had driven it home, without getting a scratch on it. JP took a moment to admire his apparent ability. He had an uncanny skill to drive while drunk. Even when he could not stand up straight, he could still drive straight. But Madison's SUV had memories associated with it. Memories he needed to leave behind.

JP's car was still down the street where he had left it the day before. As he walked to it, he realized he had abandoned it while it was still running. The door was open, and the dash was lifeless. It had run till the gas gauge hit empty, and then it had died.

JP blew air between his lips thinking and decided that bringing his car back to life would be more tedious than a few memories. He would just use Madison's SUV. Hers was bigger than his little coupe anyways. And he did not feel like searching around for a car that wasn't dead and had the keys in it. There were a few things he collected from his car, and then he said goodbye.

He packed everything he could think of—blankets, food, whiskey, cigarettes, extra lighters, bottle openers, a few magazines, and his dad's Colt 1911 pistol. When there was an item he did not have, he searched his neighbors' houses and took whatever he liked.

While in the driver's seat of Madison's car, JP noted how ordinary the houses he passed were. It was like any other day. The same lawns, the same flowers, the same doors, and the same roofs. No wonder he hadn't noticed anything was wrong on his walk back from the park. Or rather, he hadn't noticed anything more wrong than what was going on in his head. But then he came to a row of idled cars blocking the road, so he climbed the curb and scooched around them on the lawns.

And then there were the fires. Entire blocks were raging in the distance. Some houses lay now as embers, but the blaze had not spread any further. There were also many animals. Dogs and cats roamed the streets looking for food and water and trying to avoid the flames. Even the wild animals had become bolder now that the neighborhood was devoid of humans.

Of all things, JP had pity for these animals. He had always wanted a dog. But, of course, his parents had forbidden it.

Once he found his new home, he would have to search for one, a German Shepherd or something. Definitely a bigger breed. "*Who needs humans when you can have a dog?*" he thought jokingly.

Only halfway joking.

But there were people. They looked more lost than the animals. Some were hastily packing their own cars, probably with the same idea as JP. Others were going from house to house looting and gathering everything they could. Some simply sat on the ground and cried. There was at least one little group, trying to band together, trying to make sense of it all. JP was tempted to stop. Maybe he could join them? But there was one who seemed to be dictating directions to the rest, and JP didn't want to be directed, not even for his own good.

He almost stopped once. A string of houses had caught fire down a side street. Black smoke billowed up to join the smog of other house fires to create a dense cloud of soot. At the very edge of the spread, a blonde woman was leaning over a man lying unconscious on the sidewalk. Half the man's body was charcoal. But the woman was still trying to save him. JP wanted to get out and see if he could help. He didn't. He knew there was nothing he could do. Really, there was nothing anyone could do. He kept on driving.

On the freeway, there was nothing but empty cars. Some had smashed into the walls and rails and each other. Others, stalled on the asphalt, sat there waiting, waiting for a driver who would never return. A spot of rain approached from the distance. The pitter-patter on his windshield gave the sight a melancholy aura. The highway was empty. Full of cars but empty. JP turned on the Bluetooth and blasted something energetic.

He rode the freeway until he encountered a pile-up of empty cars so bad that he could only turn around and take side streets to get past it. But by then, he was nearing the country. There were flourishing soybean fields to his left and thick rows of corn stalks on his right. The rain cleared up and the sun glinted brightly. Every once in a while, he'd see horses grazing in a pen, or even out in the open.

This area was completely untouched by the disaster raging in the suburbs, probably because there were fewer people here to disappear in the first place. He kept his eyes open for his goal and stopped at the first house he saw that still had lights on. It was hard to tell in the daylight, but the fact that it had a whole array of solar panels outside gave it away.

It was a white farmhouse, with a large, covered porch out front and several medium-sized barns directly behind. It had no fields for crops, and the barns now only contained a rusted truck and a tractor for cutting the grass. But it had power, and that is what mattered.

The interior had four rooms on the first floor, and two on

the second as well as a small cellar below. The walls were painted white, and the carpets were a crisp eggshell. There were many small coffee tables and lampstands, covered with picture frames, religious ornaments, and candles, always with a layer of decorative lace between the items and the wood.

The first thing he did in his new home was shower,36houghh the soap made him smell like an old person. He'd have to find something different in one of the nearby houses. He'd have to do a lot: get nonperishable food, bottled water, maybe start a vegetable garden. But all this could come later. Right now, he wanted to celebrate his newfound freedom, not waste it on being responsible.

He checked out the cellar, hoping beyond hope for his bottle of tequila, but was not surprised to be disappointed. He emerged again with a bottle of wine in his hand. Not a bad way to celebrate. Not bad at all. But the bottle of wine was soon joined by half a bottle of the whiskey he had brought with him.

A portable speaker tied to his arm, JP wandered around the house blaring songs by Oasis and poorly singing along to them. An extremely dangerous thing to do.

Slowly, JP slipped into the midst of a nostalgia trip, which made no sense as he was not alive when Oasis was popular. The consequences of being in such a contradictory state were not good. His grasp of the past was slipping into a self-indulgent mythology.

Luckily for him, he had no memory of it in the morning, so there was no harm done. The same cannot be said for any vases and photos he found in the house. Perhaps the images of the smiling old couple offended him, or perhaps he was just really, really drunk, but as soon as he saw one, he pulled out his 1911 and shot it. It took two or three shots before his ringing ears convinced him not to do it again. But then, five minutes later, when he had forgotten his resolution, he would pull out the gun and do it again. Soon, he ran out of ammo. Then again, he was also out of vases and photos.

The next day, after recovering, he made it a point to clean up all the glass shards and patch some of the bullet holes that had gone through the walls before doing it all again. And after waking up on the third day, he sat in bed and did not want to move. Not to get drunk again anyways. And not to hurt his ears in a new way. There was no magic in it. He had been spending every night living like that for over a year, and it had never gotten repetitive. But now that he did not have school to escape from and he was not at risk of being caught by his parents, getting drunk had lost its flavor. Maybe he needed some people to share it with. They do say that there is no point in drinking alone. Not that they existed anymore. But the saying still held true.

• • •

After emptying Madison's car, JP drove around to the neighboring farms. They were devoid of people but full of supplies like food and bottled water. His own bag was filled with cigarettes he had taken from the gas station, so he dumped out Madison's pink soccer bag. Whenever he found a bottle of whiskey or wine, he'd wrap it in a T-shirt and pack it in the bag for later. But despite his keen eyes, he did not find another bottle of that authentic tequila. Not that he expected it to be in one of these country farmhouses, but not looking for it would haunt him. And JP knew that as soon as he found it, he would be satisfied. But he couldn't even find something to properly patch the bullet holes he had shot in the house. The miscellaneous objects he stuffed in them kept falling out, and now ants were crawling in.

In the bag, there was also a bottle of water, some snacks, a flashlight, and a few other emergency items. Enough to get JP through a day, as his searches were finding him farther and farther from his little white farmhouse. His third day of searching brought him onto the main street of a little country town. He was hoping to locate a liquor store, which would greatly increase his chances of finding his desired bottle. He stopped at a little sign at the beginning of the row of shops that conveniently mapped out all the businesses in the town. There was a bookstore, a pharmacy, a hardware shop, a butcher, and a coffee house, but not a liquor store.

"Where did these people get their booze!" he exclaimed. He checked the pharmacy, suspecting that a small-town drug store might sell alcohol, but if that had ever been true, it wasn't anymore.

Walking down to the town center, JP passed the coffee shop and noticed something strange there. Through the window, he could see three individuals seated around a table, steaming mugs in their hands and grins on their faces. They were laughing and smiling like it was any other Saturday. Like there was nothing weird about the disappearance of 99.9 percent of every thousand persons. There was a familiarity between them, one that could not have been formed since everyone else had disappeared. JP was struck by longing. They noticed him gawking at them, and one of them waved him in.

A bell rang as JP opened the door. It startled him out of his shock.

The one who waved him in was a woman, early twenties by the look of her. She eyed JP up and down. She smiled at him, like he was a long-expected guest she had been told the most amazing things about. "Hi, welcome. Can I get you a coffee?" She, like JP, probably had no idea what to say. Greetings had to be different since meeting someone new was so rare. On one hand, it was overwhelming, intoxicating. On the other, it was a waste of time, when both people were so curious that they'd rather be absorbed into the other than have to take the time to learn about them.

"Sure, what do you have?" JP asked. The aroma of coffee was thick in the air.

"I've got cappuccino without milk and iced without ice."

"So, just black?"

"Yeah." She laughed. "Business has been tough ever since the power went out and almost everyone vanished. All the milk spoiled, and the espresso machine doesn't work, and only two of my regulars come anymore." She indicated the other two seated at the table.

A thin man in the corner raised his hand in acknowledgement of JP but said nothing. The other man, short, middle-aged, with a receding hairline and bulging belly, pulled at his rubbery chin, considering JP.

"I guess I'll take a black, then. But I don't have any money."

"Don't worry about that. I've been handing out free cups ever since my boss stopped paying me." She got up, about to head to the counter area.

"Now hold on there," the chubby man said. "We don't even know this kid. Remember the last passer-through? He tried to make off with a case of whiskey and a bag of women's underpants. I had to chase him away with my baseball bat. How do we know he isn't a pervert like that guy?"

All three of them considered JP as if they might be able to

tell if he did nefarious things with girls' underwear by the shape of his nose or the color of his eyes.

"Well, I haven't pulled a panty raid since summer camp when I was twelve," JP said. "I led my cabin to victory with a whole fifteen pair, true story, but those days of glory are far behind me. Haven't stolen a panty since."

The woman wiped her brow. "Phew, I'm glad we got that out of the way. I can finally stop storing my underwear in a locked chest." She couldn't hold the sarcasm and broke into a grin.

"I don't know," said the man, "ole Betsy here can smell if a person's trouble." He patted the wooden bat leaning against his chair. "She's smelling something off about him."

"Oh, that, it's the old person soap I've been using. It smells awful, but it does wonders for my skin." Maybe it was the fact that this guy kept his bat so close at hand, and that it looked like it was used to hit more than baseballs, but JP felt unsettled by this chubby man and his black, beady eyes.

"Anyway, I'm Jessica." The woman held out her hand.

JP shook it. "JP," he said. Their grip lingered for a moment.

"Hold on, hold on, I'm telling you, Jess, we don't know what this kid's made of yet."

Jessica rolled her eyes. JP returned the man's suspicious stare. "And how would I go about proving myself, if you're not going to take a moment to get to know me?"

"Oh, we're going to take that moment. We're going to see if you're capable of being a part of our town."

"Toby, perhaps it would be unwise—" the thin man in the corner began.

"Shut up, Carl," Toby cut him off.

"Carlos," he corrected in a small voice, but said nothing more.

"Here's the deal, kid, if you beat the test, you can stay if you want, or you can gather supplies here and be on your way. You have free rein. But, if you fail, I'll knock you over the head with ole Betsy and take you down to the river. You'll wake up on the bank somewhere with not a chance of coming back. Got it?"

JP looked at ole Betsy and then at Toby's beady eyes. He decided that the man was very much capable of everything he described. And since he could easily find a car and drive back, JP suspected that "no chance of coming back" meant breaking his legs or something. But JP had not been able to shake the longing he felt when he first saw them in here, laughing, smiling, being normal, or what once was normal.

"Sounds fair," he agreed.

"He's not gonna—" the woman tried to reassure JP.

"Jessica," Toby said calmly, "I'll do what I must."

"What's the contest?" JP asked.

"Shots."

A grin slipped over JP's face. "Shots? Well, why didn't you say so?" He reached into his backpack and pulled out a bottle of Jack.

Toby grinned. "Oh, no—we don't play with toys," he said softy. He put his hand behind him and then tenderly placed a bottle of a clear liquid on the table.

JP's confidence waned. Was he about to do shots of Everclear?

"It's my own homemade moonshine. I use this to remove the rust off old beaters and for chasing vodka. It'll put a pair of balls on anybody."

Standing there, Jessica looked down at herself. JP got the sense that she had taken a shot of the stuff and was regretting it now that she knew what the side effects were. Then, she looked over at JP, and then down. She was probably wondering if he had any balls, and now JP could certainly not back down with the question of his manhood in the air.

"All you have to do is take three shots and not yack," Toby said. "And I'll do them with you."

"I accept," JP said, feigning a confident smile to Jessica. She returned it but shook her head.

"But what if you yack?" JP asked.

"Then I'll let you have any bottle from my personal stash. There are five-hundred-dollar bottles in there, but don't worry about that, it ain't going to happen."

"All right."

"Jessica, grab some fresh cups," Toby commanded.

As Jessica walked away, JP watched. She wore jean shorts and a red flannel, which was all tied up in the back, so it did not cover her midriff. When she got behind the counter, she tiptoed around as if the floor was covered with obstacles. Her foot knocked something, and it rolled on the ground until it clinked up against something else.

"Careful, Jessica," Toby said in a truly concerned voice.

She came back with two small cups meant to put espresso in.

JP took the fourth chair at the table and faced Toby. Gingerly, careful not to spill any, Toby filled both cups. They were larger than a double shot, and JP began to regret accepting this challenge. From the look in the chubby man's eyes, JP guessed Toby was already deliberating on what side of the head to bonk him. Jessica remained standing between JP and Toby, watching both of them and shaking her head.

The thin man, Carlos, sat silently across the table with a disapproving frown.

"Cheers," JP said. He tried to put on a smile. Toby's face was blank. They raised their cups, knocked them to the table, and downed them.

JP shook his head like someone had lit a fire within it and

then began rubbing his eyes, unable to keep still.

Toby gave a whistling "he-he." He was smiling now, a slimy upward twist of the lips.

By the time JP got control of his body movements again, Toby was already pouring the next glass. Taking a deep breath, JP prepared himself. He ran his hands through his hair to find some calm and then met Toby's beady eyes as they both grabbed hold of their cups.

The stuff JP usually drank was cheap and weak. He had no experience with moonshine, and his chest was closing up with anxiety.

Up.

 To the table.

And then down the hatch.

JP gulped after. He had control of his body movements, but things were slipping. He remembered in a horrible moment that people could die from drinking too much. He looked at Jessica's concerned face and then out the window at the empty street. It was going to be worth it. He reconnected eye contact with Toby.

JP gave his best lazy-eyed stare, which at this point was more natural than anything else. Toby's grin was open wider, probably because he was having trouble keeping his jaw closed.

Again, Toby started to pour the moonshine. When both

cups were full, the bottle was empty. They just stared at each other. Both of them had forgotten there was anyone else in the room. Toby grabbed his cup and didn't even wait for JP. He slammed the empty cup face-down on the table. He dared JP to do it. JP looked down at the cup. Cups? There were two of them, now four. They were multiplying and becoming less distinct. Don't they say moonshine can make you go blind? But that's only if you make it wrong. Toby didn't seem like the guy to screw up his alcohol.

"Crap," he muttered, unable to keep the word from escaping. He reached his hand out for the cup, knowing that once he downed it, he was going to throw up, pass out, and wake up on a riverbank. But before his hand could find the cup, Carlos had reached over and downed it. He placed it gently on the table.

"That was a stupid thing to do," Toby said furiously, slurring his words slightly.

"Yeah." JP nodded dopily in agreement while thanking Carlos vigorously in his mind.

Toby and Carlos locked eyes for a moment.

"I didn't think you'd like it if JP here threw up all over ole Betsy and the rest of us," Carlos said in a slight accent.

Toby grunted but then started laughing. "He did pretty fine. He certainly showed that he has the stuff in him."

"And for that, he gets a free coffee," Jessica said. She

walked behind the counter again and took a kettle off a gas stove.

Toby became JP's instant friend now that he had a shot or two with him. "So, what's you gonna do, kid? Wanna stay a while?"

"Oh, I don't know. I hear the coffee shop only serves black, and I don't think I can make it through the season without pumpkin spice."

"Well, there is a pumpkin patch a few miles away." Jessica returned, coffee in hand. "And I'm sure we could find some spice somewhere." Their hands brushed when she gave him the cup, and the contact lingered for a moment. JP's vision was still too blurry to read her expression, but he got the sense she was suggesting something to him.

"What's JP stand for?"

"John Philip."

"I like that name, reminds me of that football player who used to play for the Saints," said Jessica, as she twirled her black hair around her finger.

Then Toby twirled some imaginary hair and mockingly said, "I like that name, reminds me of a big, juicy steak." Jessica put on a face of indignation, but JP couldn't help but grin, and even Carlos smiled at her. He had dark, tangled locks, brown eyes, tan skin, and a verdant patch of hair growing above his upper lip. Tall but skinny, he looked unfortunately breakable, like an icicle or a house made of sticks. He didn't say anything but added an uneasy grin. Looking at this man's untended mustache, JP stroked his own blossoming facial hair, now a little self-aware.

They asked him about where he was from and what he had been doing since everyone vanished. When JP was done, he asked the same things. They had all lived in or around this town. Jessica had worked at this coffee shop. She had hated her boss and refused to go to college. They all had known each other in passing, nothing too friendly. But it was easy to become friends since they could all make fun of the same people who used to inhabit the town.

They all slept in different apartments on this stretch of road. Jessica refused to sleep in her bosses' bed, so Toby had taken the coffee shop. Within a couple of hours, JP felt like he had lived in this town all his life and had known these people for just as long. His foot brushed against Jessica's, but neither pulled away. He looked at her. She giggled at something Toby said. JP looked at all of them and smiled.

It was with this merry band of strangers JP entertained himself for the next couple of days. The town was their playground, and they were children. Even the lack of power did not bother JP in the midst of their joviality. The cares of the world could not harm them anymore. They went to the fanciest restaurant in town, one they had never been able to afford, and played pretend. They set the tables, lit candles, and dressed as fancily as they could manage. Their napkins were tucked into their collars, and they ate every bit of their canned rigatoni with different forks.

When they were finished, JP stood up and pulled the tablecloth off. Miraculously, everything but a few forks remained on the table. They laughed and clapped as JP bowed. A surprised smile was pinned to his face. Surprised because he had intended for all the stuff to fall off in a great crash.

After leaving the restaurant, JP handed each one of them a cardboard box from out of Madison's SUV. They were something he had brought from home, having missed his chance to use them while the world was still there.

He led the group to the church, and they climbed to the top of the steeple. At the top, JP opened his box and dumped its contents over the side. Hundreds of bright-colored bouncy balls scattered on the roof, and down to the street below. They cascaded around town, bounced over buildings, and even broke a few windows. The others looked at JP, a little stunned. Then, Jessica tipped over her box. Carlos began to protest, something about creating a hazard, but his plea only prompted Toby to dump his own box over the side. They all watched in amazement as the bright-colored balls hopped around their town.

When JP was back on the street, Jessica was laughing and pulling away from his advances. The other two, older and more cautious descending the decrepit steps from the steeple, were still in the church. With a clever smile, Jessica gave JP a playful push and ran over to the fountain in the center of the square. She sat on its edge, legs crossed, and let a coy expression replace her smile. As JP approached, she held out her hand. He took it. Their eyes melted into each other. And slowly, she pulled him closer. Right before their lips met, JP closed his eyes. But instead of the sensation he was expecting, he became aware he was moving and opened his eyes as he hit the water. Jessica stood over him, pointing and laughing from outside the fountain. After a moment's shock, JP grabbed her outstretched hand and pulled her in too.

That night continued much the same way. They even got timid Carlos to join in the fun at times. After the two other men had gone to sleep, JP and Jessica were alone under the moonlight. Jessica sat down on a bench in the town square and left her hand on the seat beside her. Sitting down himself, JP thought that hand looked forlorn, being all alone on the cold bench. His chest flushed with blood as he took the hand in his. The hand shuddered, as if it wanted to pull away, but it didn't. A heartbeat pulsed through it, going quicker as the hand accepted his.

JP stared straight ahead but saw nothing. The wind rustled the trees and blew in his ears, but JP only heard the thump of his heart. The only thing that existed was him and this hand. He was almost surprised when he turned and found that there was a person attached to it. For a moment, their eyes met. JP looked down at the fingers entangled in his and gripped them tighter. Once again, all that was, were him and this hand. The contact made his heart quicken, but he wanted more than just a hand. He wanted an arm, a shoulder, and all the rest—

The next evening, they went to the theater. The power was off, and the room was pitch-black, so they played verbal improv. And JP was glad of the dark because of what he and Jessica were doing while Toby tried to mimic a black pastor giving a sermon on the Rapture.

"One day, brothers and sisters, one day the Good Lord will take us all away to Abraham's Bosom and leave all the sinners here on Earth to rot."

JP and Jessica gave a loud "amen."

"On that day there will be gnashing of teeth and wailing in the streets. Only those vile nonbelievers will remain, and their very sins will consume them. The lust of their hearts will consume their flesh, and the alcohol they enjoyed so much will be poison. Excuse me." Toby took an audible swig of whiskey and then continued. They all laughed. Well, maybe they had been right about the Rapture, but JP wasn't gnashing his teeth. He was holding in a wail, but that was because Jessica had accidentally bitten his tongue.

The next two days, JP spent exclusively with Jessica. They did many things, in many places. JP spent a whole hour searching for his nice Adidas joggers in the lane behind the stores that lined Main Street because Jessica had stolen them and hidden them on a canopy that hung over the backdoor to the coffee shop. JP didn't mind terribly, since there was no one around to see him pantless. Jessica didn't talk much but was always giggling, and she knew how to communicate without words. JP appreciated that talent, but sometimes it revealed things she would rather have kept hidden.

The evening of their third day together, they went up to the roof of the butcher shop, the apartment above which JP had taken to sleeping in. It wasn't the same sight of the steeple, but it felt freeing to be up high. JP performed a little waltzing dance, arms spread like he was about to embrace the world itself. Then he tripped and nearly stumbled to the edge.

"Be careful!" Jessica shrieked.

After steadying himself and peering over the edge more cautiously, JP said, "Thanks for the advice, but in hindsight, it came a little late."

"Just be careful from now on."

"Oh, don't worry. I probably wouldn't die from this height anyway. I'd have to be trying to kill myself, and even then, there's no guarantee. Though without hospitals and doctors, I'd probably die eventually, just not from the initial fall."

She shook her head and then gave him a fake push toward the edge, clearly signifying that she was over the whole worry. They sat at the edge, letting their feet dangle in the open air, and watched as the sky turned pink and then to crimson. It was beautiful, and JP had some clever lines prepared to compare Jessica to the setting sun. But when he turned to her, her eyes and mind were far away. Perhaps in a different time. A time where the streets were busy with cars and the sidewalks were occupied by people not bouncy balls. JP let the words hang on his lips and then stared up at the sky again. He had left things in that time too, many things he cared nothing about. But at least one, he missed.

No. He could not linger in the past. He must make plans for new experiences. So, he busied himself by mapping out in his mind all the buildings he had yet to search for his precious bottle of tequila.

The following morning, JP had a longing for some more substantive conversation. So, instead of going and finding Jessica, he went and shared a cup of coffee with Toby.

"Play baseball, kid?" asked Toby.

"No, not much of a sports guy, though I can be convinced

to watch some of them."

"That's too bad. I happen to be a fairly good batter. I keep my ole Betsy right here in the coffee shop if you ever want to play a little ball." He brought out the worn wooden bat that had a strange stain on the tip like it was used to hit more things than baseballs. JP remembered ole Betsy and decided he did not want to have many encounters with her.

"I once used this bat to hit a fully loaded home run against a team of professional Filipino players. Let me tell you, those Filipinos don't have anything on homebred Americans." JP learned a lot about Toby, his average pitch speed, how he could change a car's alternator in three minutes, and the entire process of distilling moonshine. JP learned so much about him, he doubted if Toby had learned a single thing about who JP was.

One of the few questions that Toby asked was how JP got to be such a fun guy. But he meant that rhetorically. And JP didn't want to explain to Toby about the goody-goody he used to be.

After he had finished his coffee, JP searched a few of the buildings he had noted the evening before.

Nothing.

Well, not nothing, just not the tequila.

At lunchtime JP shared smoked oysters and crackers, and twinkies for dessert, with Jessica. She went off to clean her clothes and JP found Carlos.

The building Carlos had stationed himself in was an old secondhand bookstore. And every book inside was ancient and thick. JP found him sitting in a corner, nose-deep in a leather-bound book with no title on the cover or spine.

"Whatcha reading?"

Carlos jumped so hard he dropped the book. After seeing it was just JP, Carlos picked the book back up and answered. "The Summa Theologiae, second part of the second part."

"Okay," JP said, clueless. "Who's it by?"

"Saint Thomas of Aquinas, very influential theologian and philosopher."

"Oh!" JP got excited. "I remember him. He says that natures are common both in reality and the mind, though individual in reality and universal in mind."

"You know Thomas Aquinas?" Carlos looked at him skeptically.

"Only on the problem of Universals. Like, if there are things that are the same as other things." And in answer to Carlos's continued puzzlement, JP said, "You think about weird things when you're drunk. Like what are things and is that tree the same thing as that other tree or is every tree completely individual? And other thoughts like what happened to my pants. Lots of strange thoughts, really. And so, I spent a month of class time reading up on the question.

And Aquinas was one of the people who weighed in on the debate. Not that I understood much of the answers, but it was better than learning chemistry. Though I never did find those pants."

Carlos looked at him with a newfound respect. They spent a few hours talking about the subject. It struck JP that Carlos acted perfectly normal. Alone, he was not the scared, timid man he was with Toby and Jessica. JP didn't leave till after the sun had set, and Carlos said he was going for a nightly walk.

JP found himself talking with Carlos one-on-one a lot. At least whenever he had a break from *the Tigress*, which was Toby's new name for Jessica, seeing how she preyed on young, innocent JP.

But *the Tigress* was prone to boredom, or maybe loneliness. After only a short while of being parted, she would seek JP out again and they would go exploring.

While walking down Main Street with her, JP recognized a building from earlier that week. It was easily identifiable because there was a life-sized statue sitting in the window. JP suddenly burst down the adjacent alley. When Jessica caught up, she found him staring up at a fire escape off the side of the building.

"Remember how we were unable to get into that apartment up there?" he asked her.

"Yeah."

"Here, give me a hand. I'll lift you up, and you grab the ladder."

They performed this action and were soon standing on the fire escape looking into the apartment. JP put the palms of his hands to the glass of the window and pushed up. It slid open. JP stood aside and said, "Ladies first."

"Why, thank you," said Jessica, crawling through the window.

The apartment had only three rooms, a bedroom, a bathroom, and a main room that doubled as a kitchen and a living room. JP went over to the exterior door, knocking a little statue off the coffee table as he passed through the living room. He undid the bolt and unlocked the handle. Then they started looking around at things. Jessica gazed in a full-length mirror as JP searched through the cabinets in the kitchen. After hearing many disappointed sighs and seeing him move on to search a dresser in the living room half, Jessica asked JP, "So, what are you searching for?"

"I am looking for a particular bottle of tequila."

"What's so special about this bottle?" she said, frowning at herself in the mirror.

A moment passed before JP answered. "It's sort of a trophy, a reminder of who I used to be."

She looked over at him, but his head was in a large drawer. "And who was that?"

"I guess you could say I was a little bit of a rule follower, and little know-it-all on top of that."

"You? Following rules? In a world without laws, you can't even follow Carlos's one prohibition on setting random junk on fire."

"Exactly."

"Exactly what? Why does this bottle remind you of that?"

"Because stealing it was the first thing I did once I found out that following the rules doesn't matter."

"Well, you wouldn't have singed your hand if you hadn't torched the stuffed bear in city hall. So—"

Jessica looked back at the mirror, her lips pursed. This time she sighed. There was a moment when the only sound was JP rustling through shirts and coughing from the dust he was stirring up. But then he pulled his head out quickly when he heard a loud crash. He looked over at Jessica. The mirror was cracked in two. The little statue he had knocked over earlier lay beneath it, broken in pieces. It was a depiction of a man and a woman holding each other in their wedding outfits.

"What'd you do that for?"

"It works better this way."

"It's broken," JP said, coming over to her and looking into the mirror himself.

"That's right." Jessica examined herself in the shattered reflection. She nodded with approval at her alteration. JP looked at their broken images on the broken surface. He turned away and noticed the lamp on the table. He chucked it at the mirror. They began breaking everything in the apartment, giggling like naughty children.

JP threw a digital clock at the door just as Carlos came running through it. The clock bounced off the door frame without hitting him. All the same, Carlos dropped the bag of glass jars he was holding. A few of the jars cracked, and the remainder scattered on the floor with the rest of the wreckage JP and Jessica had made.

The two deviants stopped their rampage as the startled Carlos steadied himself.

"Hi, Carlos—" JP began.

"What are you two doing!" Carlos cut him off.

JP stood in silent shock. Carlos had never before raised his voice to him, or at all in general.

"What's it matter to you?" snarled Jessica, baring her tiger fangs.

"You can't just destroy things."

"Why not?" Jessica took a defiant stance, legs spread, hands on hips.

"We might need this stuff in the future. And what if you hurt yourselves? If one of these shards of glass slit the wrong artery—"

"Look, Carlos," said JP, finding his voice, "thanks for your concern, but let us worry about us. You should worry about yourself and your empty jars. But hey, if you want, we'll take our shenanigans outside of town. All right?"

Carlos didn't answer. He shook his head and began collecting his jars from the carnage. When he was gone, JP and *the Tigress* left the apartment too, leaving it in chaos. The sun was already setting, so they decided not to venture any farther that day.

When JP looked over at her, he saw that the Tiger in her had disappeared. Like a fairy tale, she had transformed from the proud hunter into a kitten. Her eyes were wide as they reflected the setting sun. He realized that the sunset had this power over her, like some magic, or a curse.

"Jessica," he said. The spell broke, and the Tigress returned, more ferocious than ever, as if it was angry to have been temporarily subdued. But her eyes were still wide like a kitten's.

Early the next day, JP walked into the bookstore. He didn't want any hard feelings between him and Carlos. He found the thin man in the backroom, clearing off a large table that had books stacked on it to the ceiling. Paperbacks, large leather-bound, multi-volume encyclopedias, magazines, and everything in between were stuffed on top and beneath it, forming a solid wall of books.

JP knocked softly on the doorframe, to announce his presence without startling Carlos, who was balancing a stack of books in his arms.

"Hey, Carlos."

"Oh, hello."

"Sorry about yesterday. I didn't think it would harm anyone." JP came closer and grabbed a stack of books from the table.

"It's fine. I only want us to be prepared for the future, to take care of the resources we have now, that we may not be able to have later."

"That makes sense. Jessica and I just got carried away, that's all." JP went to place his stack of books on a cardboard box.

"Don't put those there, please. I need that."

JP stuck the books on the ground next to the box and then unfolded the top. The box was filled with the glass jars from yesterday.

"What are you doing with these?"

"I am going to be canning some raspberries this afternoon, so we will have fruit in the winter." The scrawny man's eyes gleamed when he said raspberry.

"*He must really love them*," JP thought.

"Don't you mean jarring?"

"It's called canning."

"Oh." JP thought that they had plenty of canned fruit, but he didn't say anything.

"Hey, how about I help you out? he said instead. "I don't like raspberries, but I saw some peach trees down the road. Can we do peaches?"

"Yes," Carlos said with a smile. "We can do both."

JP was going to return in an hour, and then he and Carlos would go pick the fruit.

On his way back to the bookstore, JP heard Toby call to him. "Hey, kid, come take a look at this."

JP walked over and peered into the box Toby was pulling out of his car. "Are those grenades?"

"Found them in the back of the pawn shop down near the highway. Ever throw one?"

"No. Never seen one."

"It's easy, just like a baseball. Here." Toby tossed him one.

JP caught it with tender nervousness. He choked down his fear so Toby would not consider him a wuss. "Well, I can't do it here. I'll probably accidentally kill Carlos."

"Big loss," Toby scoffed. "But you're probably right. I don't want you to break any of my stuff."

"There's that run-down house at the end of Main, we could stand behind the garden wall and toss it in the windows."

"Well, let's put this back in the car and drive down there."

JP was about to hop in the passenger seat when his face fell. "Crap, I was going to help Carlos pick raspberries and peaches and can them."

"Carlos! What do we need more canned fruit for? There's a ton of it. Besides, it's not like there's anyone else around to pick the fruit. It will be there later."

JP thought for a second. "Okay, but I get to throw first." JP got in the car.

It started off as JP had described, throwing them over a wall at a run-down house. It ended when they tied five of them together, taped them to a wheelchair, and pushed it down a steep hill. The chair fell over after three yards, and the two men jumped to the ground as the entire thing exploded. They were both amazed to find themselves unharmed.

When JP finally found Carlos, it was already evening, and his ears were ringing.

Carlos looked up from the raspberries he was packing into a jar and said, "Was it you making all that racket?"

"What?" JP asked, unable to make out what was said between Carlos's accent and the ringing in his ears. "Sorry, I got caught up."

"It's fine," he said softly. "There are yours." Carlos pointed at the twenty jars of peaches sitting on the end of the table. He went back to his canning, but JP saw the disappointment in his movement. Disappointment in JP. There were only a few more jars to fill, but he had spent all day working on them. If JP had helped, it would have been half the time.

"Here, let me help you clean up at least." He started to clean off tools and take out the bags filled with peach pits and other garbage. They didn't talk, but JP could tell that Carlos appreciated even the little he did.

The sun had gone down, leaving the small country town basked in darkness. The stars hopped about on the black canvas and then popped behind the cloud the moon was hiding underneath. It was a dazzling night, and JP's seventh since he wandered down Main Street. They decided to have a celebration, of sorts, to commemorate a full week of being together. Something simple and more intimate than the charade they had been living. And JP accidentally decided it would be a bonfire when he dragged a few store mannequins out on the street and set them on fire. Toby set up a chair around it, and Carlos came over with a rolling office chair. Being extra, JP dragged out an old sofa, for him and Jessica to sit on.

They joked and drank and told stories of their past. Mostly, stories of the things they were glad had disappeared. No one wanted to bring up the things they actually missed about the world. Least of all JP, who was content to enjoy the cigarette Jessica passed as she snuggled up to him on the couch.

Toby went first. He started in a low, suspenseful voice. "There was a group of these devil kids who liked to play ball in the park next to my house. They always left their garbage on the grass and were constantly making noise." The chubby man went on and on about how much he hated these kids before he even told how the story got started. "I set down my whiskey and walked over to the broken window. I reached down to the pile of shattered glass and picked up the baseball. Let me tell you, those kids had no idea what was coming to them." When he was finally done, he ended his story with, "I sent those kids home crying to their mothers."

Toby grinned proudly, and JP laughed as if it were a good ending, but JP thought it was funny how this middle-aged man believed it was some achievement to beat a bunch of teenagers in a game of baseball for all the quarters and nickels they had in their pockets.

Carlos didn't laugh. Toby smirked at him. "Why don't you tell us a story then, if you think you can do better."

The thin man took a deep breath and then leaned in close. "As you may have figured out, I am not originally from this country. What you may not know is that I came here illegally."

Toby's smirk tightened into a scowl.

"When I was twelve years old, my parents were killed in a

car explosion. I had no other family, so I went to an orphanage. Being an orphan down in El Salvador was . . . difficult. Especially back then. I lived in an old mission that was originally built to convert the native peoples some centuries ago. The sisters who ran it were young and joyful, but in a year, they had grown colder, and more cautious. They had seen too many friends die, and their support was drying up. There was a time where they could only feed us once a day, and themselves only every other day. Still, they tried to teach us everything they could, so that one day we might have a future. I have never forgotten their lessons. Then, one of my best friends showed up at the door of the orphanage. He was already gaunt, and I knew I needed to get him out of there. One night I woke him in the pitch-dark, and we headed north, with only my mother's lucky machete and hope."

Jaw hanging open, JP's cigarette fell from his lips. Carlos went on to describe the trials and terror of crossing through Mexico and then the border to America. He had seen people killed, and he had almost been killed.

Toby just scowled the whole time Carlos was talking.

When it was JP's turn to tell a story, he knew he could not top Carlos's in seriousness, so his mind went to the craziest night he had ever had. The craziest night that he remembered anyways.

"It was a Friday, and in second-period gym, our whale of

a teacher had refused to let this girl leave a game of volleyball to use the bathroom. She wasn't even playing, mind you; she was just standing on the sidelines waiting to be subbed in. So, the poor girl went into a corner and peed herself, and then started crying." The firelight danced red on JP's face, as if the anger he felt about this event was as hot now as it was when it happened.

"Therefore," he continued, "later that day, me and my buddy Kyle snuck into the gym teacher's office, and what do we find in her desk but a bottle of Black Velvet, a whiskey, which looks remarkably yellow, remarkably like piss, in fact. So, we emptied the whiskey into my water bottle and filled the Black Velvet bottle up with our piss. Then we trashed the gym by scattering the equipment all over. We left and waited outside the window to her office till we heard the swearing. As we predicted, instead of cleaning up the mess, she went to her office to drown her sorrow. When she got a mouthful of piss instead, she chucked the bottle of urine at the window and shattered both.

"The best part of it, though, was that she couldn't tell the principal what had happened without admitting to having a bottle of liquor on school property. She actually had to cover up our crime so she wouldn't get fired. And then she still had to clean the gym."

Everyone was laughing, and Toby was complimenting JP

on a story well told.

Jessica leaned over. "That was a really heroic thing to do for that girl."

JP smiled at the compliment, but he wasn't done.

"No, no, that's not even the half of it." They all grew silent, eagerly wondering what could top such cosmic justice.

"Later, we gathered a group of our friends, including the girl who pissed herself, and had a bonfire on the beach, where we told them what we did. We passed around my water bottle full of whiskey and drank to that teacher's misery. But my buddy was a total lightweight and was drinking more than the rest of us. Suddenly, he just rips off his clothes and runs into the lake. We all looked at each other for a long second in shock and then we rip off our clothes and follow him in. But out of the dark, we see four figures running toward us, flashing lights. Someone had called the cops on us for lighting a fire on a private beach. None of us wanted to be arrested for trespassing, underaged drinking, and public nudity all in one night. We booked it." JP paused to let the image of a bunch of naked teenagers, sprinting through the shallows, sink in.

"We didn't even go for our clothes. I still miss that pair of joggers. We all just scattered up a hill through bushes and brambles. I had no idea what happened to the rest of my friends, but I found myself running through people's backyards, drunk as a skunk and buck naked, at two in the morning, till I realized I was on the street where my girlfriend, Madison, lived." When he said her name, JP realized he had not spoken it aloud since before she disappeared. He continued the story but in a lower tone. "I threw rocks at her window while I hid in a bush. She came out. Gave me a towel and a ride home. So, in the end, I got away scot-free."

JP went silent, and so was everyone else. They all stared into the fire, trying to ignore that JP had broken the taboo about not mentioning things they missed. Jessica's breathing was irregular, like she had become self-conscious of it and was trying to make it unnoticeable. But JP noticed.

Toby shifted in his chair. His bag was beside him, filled to the brim with packs of cigarettes, cigars, and some other stuff. He reached in and pulled out another bottle of Scotch. Packs of cigarettes poured out, but he was more concerned with ending the silence.

"Hey, Carl. Why haven't I seen you do anything brave and daring since we've been here? It's like you're afraid to have any fun. Why don't you do something to prove you're as courageous as your story suggests?"

"Like what?" a hesitant Carlos asked.

"Jump over the fire!" said Jessica, having forgotten about her breathing.

Eager to move on from the way his story ended, JP encouraged him too. "Come on, it will be fun!"

Carlos stared into the fire at the burning mannequins, a foreshadowing sign of what he feared would come.

"Come on, we're not asking you to jump in it, just over," Toby coaxed.

Desperate eyes glanced to the left and the right, but from the pressure of one's peers, there is no escape but courage, and Carlos could muster none for himself.

He rose slowly. A false smile flickered over his face as he braced himself for the stunt. Carlos locked eyes with JP for a moment, looking for help, but all he got was a reassuring grin. Turning back to the fire, Carlos sucked in one last deep breath. He took his first step. And then the second. But the third caught Toby's outstretched foot. Carlos tripped straight into and through the burning mannequins. He came out the other side hopping about, convinced he was on fire.

Jessica was doubled over with laughter. Toby pretty much fell out of his chair, he was so overcome by the spectacle. After the initial shock and seeing that Carlos was fine, JP laughed as well.

Carlos tried to be strong and laugh along at his own expense, but it died in his throat.

They were doubled over and oblivious. No one noticed the burning plastic hand that landed against Toby's bag until it had set the side of it ablaze. Toby's mouth was no longer open in laughter but clenched in rage. The plastic coverings of the cigarette packs burned quickly, engulfing the whole thing in flames.

It was pointless to attempt to extinguish the bag. Toby did not even consider it. His black eyes bulged, and he turned them on Carlos.

"You sniveling Spick!" Toby wheezed, breathing hard from fury as much as the smoke. Bottle of Scotch in hand, he swung out at Carlos's head. The glass shattered, and the remaining liquor splattered the fire, causing it to pop and simmer. Carlos crumpled. Jessica and JP went silent, but Toby wasn't done. Swearing and grunting unintelligibly, he kicked Carlos in the ribs, over and over and over again. A moan escaped Carlos with every blow, proving that he was not unconscious.

"Teach you to be more careful!"

JP stood up. "Come on, give it a rest, Toby. It was an accident. Besides, we can get you new stuff."

Toby's eyes turned to him. Firelight danced over the black pupils as if the flames were coming from within his sockets. JP let his gaze fall to the pavement. He sat back down, but Jessica echoed JP's plea. "Come on, Toby. Please!"

Toby gave Carlos one last kick for good measure before going off to the coffee shop to sulk.

On the ground, Carlos's body was twisted, and his back was arched like a frightened cat. But he did not move. Maybe it would be too painful to move. Maybe it was his instinct, to seem dead. But his chest rose and fell and rose, which convinced JP that he was alive.

Nothing.

JP did nothing. He imagined he could see two bright balls of fire looking out from the glass front of the coffee shop, just daring someone to help the beaten man.

The idiot had burned Toby's stuff, after all. Maybe he deserved it. But how could it be his fault when he was tripped? Punished for something he did not intend. But how was this JP's concern? Why should he risk Toby's ire? JP stared at a bouncy ball on the ground. Some hero he was.

The next morning JP did not want to be anywhere near Toby, nor could he face Carlos, who hadn't even made it indoors. All the wretched man was able to do was crawl his way onto the couch JP had dragged out, and he lay there still, with the rising of the sun.

The rest of them avoided the street below.

Toby went down the road to the gas station, intending to replace his lost possessions.

JP found Jessica, and they went in the other direction. The two of them loved going places they could not go before. These were not extraordinary places. But if they had climbed onto the roof of town hall when the world was still around, they might have been arrested, definitely yelled at.

They climbed up buildings, over fences, anywhere and everywhere. The world had no boundaries anymore and was theirs to do with as they willed. They played The Floor Is Lava and raced down Main by jumping from parked cars to benches to mailboxes. Thoughts of the previous night were far away in the rush of their playing. Still, a glance backward to see the immobile figure lying on the sofa would call those thoughts back in an instant.

In an effort to flee them, JP and Jessica hopped into a car and drove out into the open country, to be more truly alone.

The night was already dark, and they were too far from the town and too tired from running through cornfields all day to return. JP was driving but barely able to concentrate on the road. Jessica finished the bottle of gin they had started that afternoon in a long swig. Her face was dominated by an absent grin, but her eyes were off in the darkness. JP nearly swerved off the road while trying to watch her with the corners of his eyes. She did not react as he corrected the car. She frowned, but that came from the blackness, or what she saw beyond it.

"Hey," he said.

Looking at him, she smiled as if nothing was wrong. But

JP knew better. She never talked about it, but someone had disappeared with the rest of the world and left a giant hole in her heart. That hole came to the surface with the setting sun and often lingered till morning. He knew the feeling. He wanted to give her some reassurance. But the gin was having an effect, and the words were getting jumbled in his head. So, he said, to buy time, "Let's stop and spend the night in that farmhouse with the Halloween decorations already out that we passed earlier."

"Sure," she said.

She got out of the car first and picked her way toward the door. And as he watched her, the words he wanted came to his mind.

Words like: "The world might have disappeared, but I'm going to stay here with you." They sounded cliché, cheap, but somehow, they were what he knew she needed to hear. Maybe they were even what he wanted to say.

He called out, and she turned back to him, that mix of excitement and masked melancholy on her face. In a few steps, he caught up to her, a whole mountain of those words on his tongue. His mouth opened to say them, but it was closed by a kiss.

What could he do? Right? He kissed back.

They climbed the porch entangled in each other, bumping into chairs and knocking over a plastic skeleton. Maybe she didn't want words. Maybe she just wanted to forget. Maybe he wanted to forget too. Forget that his dreams were filled with pink soccer bags. Forget that those words should have been said a long time ago, but to a different person. But they were neglected, as they were being neglected now.

JP broke away, grabbing the door handle. The door was unlocked, and he opened it ceremoniously. Waving his hand, he stepped aside. "My lady first." Her scent intoxicated him as she brushed past. It was all he could think of. All he wanted to think of.

They stopped when something clamored in the house. Jessica jumped behind JP, and they looked warily through the open door. It was all black inside. Blackness and a clamoring noise.

The flashlight JP fished from his pocket illuminated the entrance hall. Another crash came from deep in the house. Was there someone in there? JP called out, "Hey, anybody here?" Jessica shrank back further.

No answer. A consistent pitter-patter echoed on the wood floor. If it were a person, they would have answered, unless they were insane or had rabies or something. It grew closer and closer. JP's heart began to quicken until it matched the ferocity of the approaching pitter-patter. He wanted to run, but Jessica was right behind him, blocking his escape. A vague shape burst into the light and through the open door.

JP did not realize it was a dog till it had its jaws wrapped around his leg. He fell backwards, knocking Jessica to the ground. The beast was tearing at him, trying to get away with a chunk of his calf. His jeans were shredded, and blood was spattering around him. His blood.

It pulled and pulled and ripped and ripped, snarling and growling in its throat. But its throat was filling up with blood. JP's blood. So, the growling sounded more like gurgling, which made it comical. One whole big comedy. No one really gets hurts in comedy. All the bad stuff is funny. Like when Moe pokes Curly in the eyes or Bugs Bunny blows up Elmer Fudd. But it did not feel very funny. It felt like a dog had its teeth in his flesh and was trying to tear some away.

JP's mind filled up with blinding-red panic. He kicked it twice with his free foot, but to no avail. Jessica was screaming and crawling away along the porch. Someone else was screaming too! It must have been him. But all he could do was grope around in blind hope. In blind fear. Finally, his hope was affirmed. A deck chair. He grabbed it with both hands and lifted it up above his prone body. As tears streamed down his cheeks, JP let it down, and the chair shattered on the savage. With a howl, almost mimicking JP's own screams, the starving dog let go of his leg and retreated into the doorway. It snarled and bared its dripping crimson fangs.

A great, agonized yell burst from JP as he raised himself

onto his unravaged leg. He placed both hands on the screen door and slammed it shut. The glass bottom of the door was pulverized on impact. And so was the dog.

It lay there, looking normal enough, besides JP's blood still gushing from its mouth. It was savagely hungry, probably from being stuck in an empty house for the past week and a half. Now it lay limp in a pile of bloody glass, and JP hoped it was dead.

As Jessica helped JP down the porch steps and into the passenger side of the car, he kept thinking over and over, *"I always wanted a dog."* Man's best friend was still an animal, though. At least a man can generally be trusted not to eat you. Or at least, he has the choice not to, if he's starving. *"But I always wanted a dog."*

Jessica stopped the car at the very next house; one they had explored earlier that day. She helped him into the house, and he started to say out loud, "I always wanted a dog." On the couch, JP looked at his torn leg, hysterically interested in the holes it now possessed. Searching the house, Jessica found some gauze and a tube of Neosporin. It was the best she could do, and still, JP's leg would not stop bleeding. Thin blood, from a constant use of alcohol, and current use of it, for that matter. The pain, the alcohol, and loss of blood befuddled his mind till JP passed out.

3

Consciousness is not lost pleasantly. And when it is found again, it is like a gale, appearing from nowhere, and introducing itself by delivering a sharp gust of rain-riddled wind to the face. At least, that was JP's experience of waking many mornings—correction, many afternoons, after an intense night of debauchery. Those awakenings were usually accompanied by what must have been all of existence weighing down on his head. This time, however, felt more like all existence had been drained away from him. He felt light. Empty throughout his body. Except for his left leg, which all of his being seeped down into. It created an agonizing pressure like being nailed down to a wooden board.

His first thoughts were muddled fears of being chewed out for missing school again. But then he remembered, there was no school anymore. Ash and melted metal were all that was left of that. The throbbing sear of his leg reintroduced the memory of the attack.

Was he safe?

Would he still die?

Maybe he contracted rabies.

Where was the dog?

It was dead.

Who was this girl standing over him?

Madison!

Not this time.

A different girl was here, fear on her pale face. Not the knowing disapproval and awkward smile he had woken to so many times.

This was Jessica. Jessica from after the world.

The panic slowly subsided.

"You're safe, you're safe. How are you feeling?" she asked.

"Jessica!" he said.

"Yes?"

"I—"

But he had nothing to say to her. Even when JP had woken up in beds that were neither his, nor his girlfriend's, he always thought of Madison. Even if those thoughts were filled with guilt. But he would never wake up next to Madison again.

He looked down at the reddish-brown that soaked the wrapping around his leg and then looked up at Jessica. Through Jessica.

"I could use a drink," he said with a painful, sorrowful grimace.

"Heck no! Doesn't alcohol thin your blood? I barely was able to stop the bleeding."

"Are you a doctor?" JP asked in a vicious voice.

"No."

"Then get me a damned drink!" he shouted.

"Get it yourself!" Her words and expression were a mixture of hurt and worry. She thought she knew better than him, but there are things worse than death. Thoughts, for example. Thoughts of regret. Like the ones he had just woken up with.

"Go get Toby!" he ordered through clenched teeth. She obeyed, leaving him a bottle of water and a granola bar. He munched the snack resentfully.

The house was dusty. Without people moving about, the grime had started to settle. The world had vanished, and there were still people who tried to control him. And Jessica, of all of them?

The resentment faded as he reflected on his limb. He

probably would never walk right again. Maybe Toby would have to cut it off. What did it matter if people tried to control him if he already lost his freedom to infirmity?

A scream was welling up deep in JP. A scream of pain, yes, but also of despair. For the first time, he mourned the loss of the world. A world full of ambulances and paramedics and doctors and people and Madison. There were no cares in that world, nothing really to worry about. He used to pretend being grounded was the end of the world. Now, he wished the end of the world was just a bad grounding; two weeks and then everything would go back to normal. But he expected the world would go back to normal as much as he had expected it to end, which was not at all.

Happy thoughts, JP. Happy thoughts.

He tried to think of anything but the mounting desolation, but nothing would come. "Okay, just think about how badly your leg hurts, and it will keep your mind off how ruined your life is," he told himself, but for some reason, this did not help.

Through the doorway, JP could see into the kitchen. He spotted something sticking out of a wine rack above the sink. It was a clear glass bottle, half filled with a golden liquid. He sat there staring for several minutes. It was all the way above the sink. He'd have to stand on his tippy-toes to reach it. A branding of pain shot through his leg. It was at once his greatest motivator and hindrance for getting that bottle.

Gingerly, he lowered himself off the couch. He yelled when he let his leg fall onto the pillow he had placed on the ground. He scooched backwards on his butt, dragging his hurt leg on the cushion. In the kitchen, he looked up at the cabinet. It appeared a lot higher now that he was on the ground beneath it. He tried to hoist himself up using the granite counter, but white dots cluttered his vision, and he let himself down before everything turned black. He breathed for a second, the pain so intense he was barely aware that he had a leg at all.

He tried to think, but the pain was drowning everything out, which was actually what he wanted. But this recognition only brought back the thoughts of despair. In turn, he was reaffirmed in his need to get that bottle. He scooched along the kitchen tile and grabbed the broom and the mop from the corner. Using these instruments, he wiggled the bottle to the edge of the rack. He prepared himself to catch it and dreaded that it might hit the countertop and shatter.

After dropping the mop, he gave the bottle one last tap with the broom and then watched it tilt over into midair. He flung the broom aside and reached out with eager hands. He caught the bottle and held it up in triumph. Uncorking the top, he brought it to his mouth. Mouth half full, he spit the liquid out and chucked the bottle against the opposing wall.

He swore out of frustration and out of pain because he

jerked his leg when he spit out the golden liquid. He spat and spat, trying to eliminate the rest of the olive oil.

He sat there, leaning against the sink. Unwilling to crawl back to the couch in the living room, his eyes stared at the opposing wall. They stared at the doorway he had dragged himself through. They stared.

The sun seeped low in the window. JP realized that an entire day had passed since he had been bitten. Or maybe it was several days, for all he knew. At this time yesterday, his life was being torn to shreds. He wouldn't be able to climb around town with Jessica anymore. She would become his nurse more than his lover. That is, if she stayed. He would not. They had no commitment to each other. Nothing bound them. There were no bonds left, not for country, not for God, not for marriage, at least not for JP. He had never committed to a bond.

They made him feel trapped—his school, his parents, the state, his girlfriend. That's why he did not give them a second thought when they were gone. Except that last one. Maybe he had wanted that bond. But Hot Lips came to mind. Maybe he hadn't wanted it enough to change for it. Now, he wished he had.

The house was dark now. His reflections had seemed to darken with the closing day. Now they were as black as crude oil and just as sticky. With every thought, the pain of his leg intensified. The dark house was filled with loathing. Loathing for being so alone.

Alone. That's how he always wanted it. Right? No one to control him, no one to annoy him, no one to expect anything from him. Alone.

This solitary independence was supposed to be better. It was supposed to make him happy. But happiness was out of reach. He tried to find it in drinking, in smoking, in sex. They were his pursuit of freedom, but then he would sober up. The buzz would fade. The pleasure would end and be as if it had never been. Freedom is a lonely place. And there is no happiness in being alone. But at least it was his loneliness. Right?

"Dammit," he swore, "she could have at least left me a cig!"

A soft wind brushed the pines outside. Birds called to each other, wishing everyone one final good night. And the bugs sang a drowsy song, like a lullaby, to the world fast falling asleep.

"How unjust," JP thought as he drifted to sleep, *"that the night out there is so at peace, while in here, my mind seeks to destroy me."*

JP woke to the sight of headlights shining through the window.

The door swung open, and there was Jessica, holding a flashlight, and Toby right behind her. Toby came right over. "Okay, let me take a look at it."

He did not look at JP's face, which made JP feel like a machine, and Toby the annoyed engineer who had to fix the busted thing.

"Can you feel your toes?"

"Yes." JP gave them a wiggle.

"Well, since you stopped bleeding, your main worry will be infection. There's a pharmacy down on Main. We can get you some antibiotics there. The bone is probably not broken, and other than that, I can't say much. Hopefully, the tissue is intact and heals right."

"Thanks."

"Yeah, Jess will replace your bandage, and then we'll carry you out to the car." Toby stood up with a yawn. It was late, and he had probably been woken from a deep sleep. But JP got the impression that his injury bored Toby.

When the morning light lifted JP from his sleep, he realized he was in his bed. At least, the bed in the apartment over the butcher shop. The covers were nicely tucked in all around him, and Jessica was asleep in the chair beside him. Her sleeping face wore a worried frown. Gratitude welled up in JP. It was so picturesque. Except, in all the movies, it is the man in the chair having spent all night watching over the girl, not the girl watching over JP's sorry ass. He was taken by an urge to wake her. To thank her. But a sleepy mumble escaped her lips. JP craned his head to listen.

"Michael. Where are you, Michael? I'll wait for you. Where we met, under the setting sun. I'll wait."

The smile that had been growing on his face withered. Well, now he knew who she saw in the sunset. From his story, she knew the name of his girlfriend.

Ex-girlfriend?

That felt wrong. They had never broken up. Why should she be his ex if she had disappeared for some reason beyond their control?

But here he was messing around with Jessica.

Messing around. That was all it was, wasn't it? At least to him. And for her, she was trying to forget Michael. He knew that before he knew his name, and yet, he chose not to say anything. He chose not to give her something better.

JP closed his eyes and slept, or pretended to sleep, till she was gone.

JP wakes up to the sound of Old Iron Rods, his name for his mother. She's yapping and telling him to get up for school as she throws open the curtains. JP shrinks back under his covers at the sight of the hated light. He groans and gets out of his bed after his mother shuts the door behind her. Yawning, he picks up his phone. It is only 7:20. He has another fifteen minutes he could have slept. But the phone begins to buzz, and Madison's name pops up on the screen. He answers it excitedly. "Madison!" he begins.

"JP—Hey, JP, I brought you dinner, kid." Toby tore JP away from his daydream. "Here, eat up." Toby placed the tray on the bedside table and then left. It was canned beans and a granola bar. Toby hadn't even stayed long enough for JP to say, "thank you." But JP was grateful at least, to be disturbed out of this daydream. It wasn't exciting, and it definitely wasn't helping.

The next couple of days JP spent wishing that the town had power. Then at least he might have been able to watch a movie. But as it was, there was nothing to do. On the third day, Jessica brought him a Gameboy. There was only one game, and after the first hour of playing it, he was bored again.

The more time he spent in bed, the less and less Jessica spent with him. He did not blame her, or maybe he did. Maybe she ought to stay. It would be good. Wouldn't it be? He really did not know, but something inside of him believed it was true, and that if someone else was in the same position, maybe he ought to do the same.

When JP's battery died, he chucked the Gameboy at a wall. At that moment, Carlos was coming into the room and lost control of the stack of books he had in hand. The novels toppled to the ground with the pieces of the pulverized gadget.

"Sorry, didn't know you were coming in."

"No matter."

Carlos still had a large welt on the crown of his head. He bent down and collected all the books. Placing them on the bed stand, he said, "I thought you might enjoy these, since you seemed to be interested in philosophy."

"Uh, sure," JP said, avoiding Carlos's eyes. "I really only got into the one topic, but I'll give it a try."

"Most of these are modern and short, but I had to sneak in some Plato too." He held up a dusty paperback entitled *The Symposium.*

"Thanks."

"Don't mention it." Carlos turned to leave.

"Hey, Carlos."

"Yes?" He turned back.

"Sorry I didn't make more of an effort to see if you were all right. I got caught up with Jessica. I should have been there for you."

"Don't worry about me, just rest up." Carlos turned to the door again. "Thank you, though," he said and left.

JP picked up the book Carlos had pointed out. It was about a drinking party, and about love.

The pile of books Carlos brought had grown smaller and smaller as JP went through them. Some of them he read and liked, but scattered on the floor around his bed were the ones that were too confusing or boring. The one he was reading now felt like it was going to end up on the floor. All that had happened so far was a dude went to a nursing home to bury his mother and didn't seem to care too much about it.

Out of his open window, JP heard shouting. Curious, he gingerly rose and hopped on one foot to see who it was. Toby was standing below, red-faced and gesticulating madly. The chubby man was looking down the street. The object of his frustration was, of course, Carlos, who was pulling a life-sized stone statue into the middle of the road. It was a replica of one of those famous Renaissance pieces. The poor man was clearly only doing this at Toby's behest. But Toby was less than satisfied with the job. Scattered around Toby were a few boxes of paintball gear. And he was having Carlos set up the target. A heavy target.

JP spotted Jessica off to the side, sitting in a lawn chair and sipping some coffee. She just sat and watched the verbal abuse quite passively, as if it were perfectly natural for one grown man to call another grown man a whore for bookworms and threaten to burn down his home.

As JP was watching Jessica, she attempted to stifle a laugh. Toby had gotten sick of waiting for the target to get set. He had picked up one of the paintball guns and started shooting. At first, Carlos pranced about, trying to avoid getting hit, but Toby's shots were narrowing in, and Carlos was being painted green. Carlos collapsed into the fetal position. The green pellets kept flying. Where Carlos used to be, there was now a miserable bush that ought to've stood up for itself or at least have run.

The gun ran dry, but Toby wasn't finished. He bent down and scooped up a few bouncy balls and dropped them in the hopper. Carlos's back arched backward when the first one hit him. JP looked away. He crawled back into his bed, pulled up the covers, and opened the book again.

Tired of lounging around his room, JP started to think of ideas that would get him mobile again. He mourned the fact that he and Toby had blown up the only wheelchair in town, and his first ideas were conceived out of a desire to replace it. One such idea was to duct tape a bunch of cushions to a skateboard till it was high enough to rest his knee on. This way he could roll around Main Street without using his bad leg. When Jessica brought the required objects, well, it went poorly. It was a bad idea. His leg wasn't broken or sprained, it was torn up by a dog.

After this went wrong, JP gave up on riding around town, and his next idea was crutches, which should have been his first. Jessica found a pair, and with a little effort, he was out of bed and hopping around Main Street.

Ecstatic about getting out of his stuffy room, JP burst into song. It was a glee that took both Jessica and JP by surprise. They had a little celebration that morning. Toby joked around, and even Carlos came, though he remained standing, for the welts on his back and butt prevented him from sitting.

Toby had been bored since JP got hurt. Jessica was too far away in her mind or her past; it made Toby uncomfortable. Clearly, he did not cherish time spent with Carlos, and certainly Carlos loathed getting shot by a paintball gun. But now that JP was walking around, although timidly, Toby invited him to play a game he had invented. They went out to a little bridge that ran over a small river. While JP hobbled over to the middle of the bridge, Toby pulled a cardboard box and a baseball bat out of his car.

"Here," Toby said, handing JP a grenade from the box.

"Wait, what?"

"You stand here, and I'll be over there. You pull the pin and pitch it to me."

"But what if I miss!"

"If you miss, kid, it will fall in the water, or I'll jump in the water. One way or the other, I'll be fine."

JP shook his head as if to say, *If you die, it's not my fault.* He didn't bother arguing. It was Toby's life at risk, not his.

Toby got in position, and said, "Give me an easy underhand, okay?"

"Oh no," JP said to himself as he wound up for the throw. As soon as the grenade left his fingers, JP had a terrible thought, what if Toby hit the grenade right back to him? He thought of jumping to the ground, but if the grenade landed there, he was dead, and same issue if he jumped in the water. His insides would be turned to jelly from the shock wave.

Horror seized JP as he watched Toby swing. The grenade slammed sideways and down into the still river below. Shockwaves reverberated across the water when the explosive burst. "Now *this* is baseball!" Toby shouted. He looked like a jubilant little kid, a chubby, jubilant little kid.

"Let's try another," Toby yelled, retaking his stance at the edge of the bridge.

When it was JP's turn to hit, he took the bat and hobbled over to the place where Toby had stood. He did not fancy saying no to Toby while the chubby man held either his baseball bat or a grenade.

First, he tested his balance with his bum leg. He set down his crutches next to him and gripped the wooden bat with both hands. His fingers trembled. Maybe he needed a cigarette. Maybe he needed to walk away, but he preferred to be on

Toby's good side. He didn't even like him that much, but he liked being liked by Toby as opposed to being despised by him, as Carlos was despised by him.

JP tightened his grip. Teeth clenched in an effort to ignore the pain he was causing in his leg, he stared at a grinning Toby.

"Ready?"

"Ready," JP replied in a breath. Toby wound up and then underhanded it to him. Eyes closed tight, JP swung. He felt the bat make contact and opened his eyes to see the grenade explode over the water.

"Attaboy, JP!" Toby shouted in triumph. "Like the son I never had."

"Hit me again," JP said, a fervor growing in him. An energy that had been building up inside his chest for the entire period he was locked inside his apartment. Toby smiled and got out another. He pitched. JP hit it even farther. He'd never played baseball, but something was coming over him.

"Again."

Toby wound up, but this time when JP made contact, the object shattered. Toby hadn't thrown a grenade at all; it was a glass jar. "You're on a roll," Toby said, grabbing another jar from the box. JP gazed at the red goo dripping down the bat. He gazed at the raspberry jam he had pulverized.

"Hey!" Toby yelled at him, drawing his attention back to the pitch. When Toby threw it, JP hit it. He shattered jar after jar, until the box was empty.

Toby had been right in the first place. There was plenty of canned fruit around.

"Now, that's how you make jelly," said Toby, taking his bat from JP. The red goo had seeped down to the handle, and now JP's hand was sticky with it. He tried to wipe his hand on his pants, but a red spot remained that he could not scrub out.

Toby wiped some of the red jelly off with his finger and licked it. "Not bad. Maybe Carl was right about this canning fruit thing."

JP shuddered in disgust.

"What's wrong?"

"I don't like raspberries."

Toby went in for a nap, and Carlos hid away in the corner of his book shop.

It was just JP and Jessica and half the day still left.

"Want to go exploring?"

"I don't think I am quite up to that yet. I still can't put very much pressure on this leg."

"How about a walk?"

JP nodded, and they went for a nice quiet stroll down Main Street. It felt good just to move. It felt good to have the sun on his shoulders. It felt good to have Jessica with him. He took a deep breath and lingered in that moment. Moments like this one, contrary to popular belief, don't last forever. But they are of such quality that anyone would be glad just to have had one. This moment came to a screeching conclusion when a car zoomed by the intersection close to the two of them. It was so sudden, so unexpected, that he had to take a second to make sure it was real.

JP and Jessica looked at each other. "That wasn't one of us," they said in unison.

They ran to the middle of the intersection. Well, Jessica ran, and JP managed a quick hobble. Standing in the center of the street, they started to yell and wave their hands. JP rested on his good foot and the opposite crutch. He waved the other crutch high, with a hope that the driver might look in the rearview mirror.

After a long moment, the car slowed. Taking a U-turn, it came toward them, cautiously, as if the driver feared they were phantoms, some sort of illusion made to lead him into a trap.

There were two of them, a man and a woman. They parked the car and walked over. Their names were Soren and Catherine. *"What beautiful names,"* JP thought.

Gorgeous, glorious names. Names that belonged to real people. New people. It is an extraordinary thing, to meet someone new, when you have talked to only three people for the longest time. There were periods, mostly when JP was grounded, that he only talked to his parents and maybe a neighbor for an entire week. But at least then he could look out his window and see people. There is a great deal of comfort that comes from knowing that people are there. There is an equally great deal of discomfort that comes from knowing that people are not where they ought to be.

They blew through the pleasantries; they seemed wrong to linger on. JP wanted to know everything about these two.

"We're heading to my uncle's up in Appalachia. He's the only one we knew that is still around. But the freeway's all blocked up, so we detoured through the town," the man explained.

"Appalachia? Why would you go to him?" As far as JP knew, Appalachia was a country slum, a mountain of poverty. "Why doesn't he come to you, or maybe meet you somewhere nice in the middle?"

"Well, he's a war vet and he lost a leg. He can't exactly get around, so we're going up there to take care of him."

JP looked down at his own injured leg.

"And you two knew each other before *the Vanishing*?" Jessica asked.

"That's a good name for it. *The Vanishing!* We've just been saying mysteriously *that day*, but yeah, we worked in the same building. One moment it's bustling with activity, we looked down at our work, and then it goes entirely quiet.

When we lifted our heads, we were the only two people left on the floor, and in the entire building. Which was funny because I had been working her at the water cooler for about a month."

The woman laughed and said, "Luckily for him, every other eligible man disappeared, because let me tell you, accounting jokes are really bad."

"What? You didn't like the one about the two accountants getting robbed?"

"Where the one pays back the money he borrowed just for it to get stolen?"

"Yeah. That's a classic."

"You told me that one when I asked about the stapler I loaned you."

"I did give it back."

"After everyone disappeared, and I didn't need it anymore." Catherine laughed, and Soren pretended to not understand what was wrong with that.

The two traveled light, having three bags between them in an old Toyota. They stood side by side, shoulders pressing together. For some reason, this struck JP. They seemed to be connected. Adjoined. It was not the active connection he had seen so many times, that he had lived. He would have put his hands on her shoulders or held her to himself. Anything to make it clear that she was his. But these two did not appear to claim each other, they simply appeared to be one.

Mouth hanging slightly open, JP marveled at them. They were talking about how difficult things had been with such—what was the word—*joy* in their voices. They were going to one of the poorest regions of the country to take care of an old cripple who probably needed help using the bathroom, and they still had joy.

A seed fell into his thoughts as they talked. The seed grew into a tree when they departed and produced fruit. That fruit was envy. The day had passed as they talked. JP hadn't even mentioned Toby. Maybe he hadn't wanted to share the newcomers with him. Maybe he hadn't wanted to scare the newcomers off. And Carlos, JP could not think of Carlos without being overwhelmed by some emotion that he would not face. It might have been pity, or maybe shame. But whatever it was, he could not bear to feel it.

They watched the car disappear into the fading light, and Jessica spoke.

"They were really great. I wish they could stay."

"More people are more fun," JP said without enthusiasm.

"I guess I understand, though, taking care of his uncle and all that. My uncle's a war vet too. Served in Vietnam. But he didn't lose his legs."

"Cool."

"But it's about to be night anyway, and they're nowhere near Appalachia yet. They might have at least stayed till morning."

"They probably thought they needed to make up the time they lost talking with us."

"I just wish they could have stayed. Catherine's so joyful, it's adorable, and Soren, he reminds me of someone I once knew."

"It's probably best he didn't stay, then."

Jessica turned to him, eyes wide with surprise. "Why do you think that?"

"It's hard enough to forget about the past as it is. We don't need a walking, talking reminder of the things we don't have."

"Oh." Jessica lowered her eyes and said no more.

Jessica wandered off to find a new comfort. A comfort other than him.

Alone under the rising moon, JP needed his own distraction. He found a bottle, found a roof, and surveyed and blamed the world under the night sky. It was only the shadow of the world, and yet he found it blameworthy.

Days blurred together for JP. Or maybe he was too drunk to realize only one day had passed. None of the others came near him—not even Jessica—and he did not go near them. The four walls of his room above the butcher shop were enough for him. At least, until he reached down into his bedside cabinet and came up with an empty bottle. The booze was all used up. But what did he care? The booze didn't make him happy.

There was only one bottle now that would, that special bottle of tequila. Even if it turned out to taste like crap, having it would be enough. It would mean having won. Being free. Or something.

The buildings around town did not have it. He had spent much of his time looking in cabinets, above fridges, and under beds. But most of them had already been cleared out by Toby before JP even arrived.

Toby.

The name stuck in JP's mind. Toby had cleared them out.

Maybe Toby had the bottle. His stash of liquor was considerable.

JP's mind hung on this thought.

Toby.

JP had no choice. His will would not consider any other way. Already sobering, he felt a desperate need, if not that bottle, he still needed something to see him through the night. And every bottle of booze within walking distance was in Toby's cafe. He stood up and looked out his window.

It was a warm night, and Toby was sleeping in a hammock strung between a pole and the coffee shop. He wouldn't even be in the building.

There was nothing for it. There would be no better opportunity than this. Every possible consideration was made. Even if it was made under a heavy influence of alcohol.

His shoes JP left behind, lest they sound too loud as he crossed the street. He threw on a backpack and grabbed his crutches but did not spare a thought for turning back.

JP, as quietly as his injured leg would allow, snuck across the street and down the alley behind the shop. He had spent so much time thinking about how to get in and out that the alcohol had worn off completely. Clearheaded, he remembered that the front door had a bell. But he hadn't wanted to get in through there anyway. He had discovered a back door when he and Jessica explored the alley behind that strip of shops. Jessica had mentioned that the door to the serving area opened from the backroom, but that her boss had disappeared with the key on him. Which meant if JP could get into the backroom, he could get into the main room.

So much of his plan relied on luck. He knew the back door was locked, but he also knew there was a window beside it. When he got there, he skillfully removed the screen and then pressed his rubbery palms to the glass. He pushed.

"Yes," he exclaimed in a whisper as the window slid upward. JP lifted himself carefully through the opening. Gingerly, he let his good foot onto the dark floor. He reached back through the window and retrieved one of his crutches. The other he left there for his journey back.

There was no light but the little star shine that glittered in from the window. He braced himself on a counter and felt for obstacles with his good foot. Very slowly, he made his way through the dark. Still, his foot hit something, which rolled across the room, clanging and banging the whole way. Frozen, JP listened. He imagined seeing Toby's fat face outlined by the star light streaming in through the window. There was no way he could outrun him. JP would probably get beaten within an inch of his life like Carlos had. After several minutes passed and he heard no indication that Toby had woken, JP breathed and continued his slow path to the door of the serving area.

Every time the thought of turning back popped into his head, JP immediately countered with a routine defense.

It's too late now. It's not even that bad. Toby would understand anyway. The man's snores are so loud, I could probably knock down a building next to him and it would not wake him.

Yet something in JP kept bringing up the desire to forget the whole thing.

JP twisted the handle of the serving area door. It opened. He tried to twist the knob on the other side, to make sure he could get back out, but it would not turn. Crap. He needed the key to unlock it, and he would have to go out the front if he let it close. He took off his pack and pulled out the only thing he did not need, the boring book Carlos had given him. He never understood why Carlos had suggested it. Sure, he had only read the first third, but nothing happened except the dude went to his mother's funeral and did a bad job of it. He stuck it between the door and the frame and gingerly let the door fall into place.

The dim light that streamed in from the window illuminated the room. Now able to see, JP could move quicker, but he could also see Toby, swaying gently in his hammock. He could tell Toby was asleep by the way his arm dangled off the edge of the hammock, but the notion that he might wake up at any moment and see JP digging through his stuff like a raccoon on trash day was terrifying.

Taking a deep breath, he turned from Toby and spotted his target. The entire area behind the counter was filled with bottle after bottle of booze. And it was not your Jack and Jim but some exceptionally fine liquors. Toby wouldn't even notice a few missing bottles.

Getting low to search the bottles with a busted leg was not easy. He could not crouch, and kneeling wouldn't do either, so he had to sit on his bum. He did not feel safe sitting on the cold tile. There was no easy way to get up again, so if he needed to move fast, he was screwed.

JP's eyes started hurting. He was squinting in the dim light, trying to read labels. A Weller Antique 107—that's pretty fine stuff. He wrapped it in a T-shirt so it wouldn't clank and put it in his bag. Toby had plenty. He wouldn't miss one or two bottles. He continued down the line, examining every bottle till he was sure it wasn't his tequila. JP did not rely on the unique handle to distinguish the bottle. He figured it might be possible there was a version that did not have it. After nearly twenty minutes, with only a few pauses to check that Toby still slept, JP had gone through nearly all of them. His eyes were burning and so was his leg. Both legs, in fact. The other hurt from the positions he put it in to make the busted leg feel better.

While he was trying to discern the name of a bottle by holding it above him, a light flashed over his head. He froze, then slowly lifted his head above the counter. Toby lay undisturbed.

Maybe it was nothing. If nothing else, though, it was a reminder that he had to go.

He only needed to check a few more bottles, though. Still, if someone was out and about on the street and they woke up Toby—

It didn't matter anymore. He just had to know.

Instead of going quicker, it took JP double the time to read each label. He should have known it wouldn't be here. It was not domestic. Imported from Mexico. The only reason he had gotten it in the first place was because he stole it. But now he needed it. He had stolen it that first time to prove something. To prove that he was free.

Free. Without that one deed, he would not have had the

confidence to change, to take control of his life, to get Madison. He would have been stuck. He would have ended up a victim. A victim like Carlos. A good guy, maybe, but the prey for men like Toby. The prey for men like JP.

Old memories danced before JP's eyes. They blurred his already-diminished vision, so he spent three minutes staring at the same bottle. And then another three. He could not comprehend it. Or maybe he could not believe it. Here it was. The very one. Brown bottle, blue label. He grabbed it with tender hands. He held it up to the light sprinkling in from the window and confirmed the word stamped on the cork, Viva. It even had the right handle; it was just hard to spot because of the way it had been angled.

Another flash streaked in from outside, and JP clutched the bottle to his chest. Quickly, he wrapped up his prize and stuck it in his bag. The corners of his lips were breaking new heights, he was so excited. After a peek out the window to be sure Toby was still asleep, JP opened the serving room door, slipped through, and quietly closed it.

It was awkward stumbling in the dark to the window. The counter he had leaned on before was on the other side of him, and he needed to support himself with the crutch on that side. But whatever he had knocked over on the way in was not in his path this time, and he made it to the window without a sound.

On the outside, JP shut the window, making more of a squeak than he would have liked. After the screen was replaced, he grabbed his other crutch and hobbled into the dark. Sneaking far down the alley, he peeked his head out onto Main, checked that no one was around, and then made his hurried crossing. He had gone far past the butcher shop in order to make sure Toby could not see him walking across the street, and now had to walk back toward it knowing that he was also walking back toward Toby.

A pack of thick clouds had floated in front of the star light, casting everything into a dense void. JP could not see Toby in the dark, which hopefully meant that Toby could not see him either. Part of JP wished he could see Toby, because he now imagined him right beyond the veil of every shadow. JP looked up at the shop he was in front of. It was the bookstore, which meant his apartment was only two more down.

He picked up his pace, keeping his eyes trained in the direction of the coffee shop. His foot landed on something round. A bouncy ball. He started to fall back but threw himself forward so he wouldn't fall on the bottles. His crutches tumbled to the pavement, clattering loudly. He sniffed the concrete and suppressed the groan that was rising to his lips.

A beam of light enveloped JP. It froze him, as if it were shot from a ray gun or stun weapon. Now, instead of the dark, he was blinded by the sharp light and red fear.

"What are you doing?" said a quiet voice from beyond the light.

Carlos.

"Turn that off," JP snapped. Carlos obeyed. JP found his crutches and rose. He turned to the coffee shop, but the flashlight had destroyed what night vision he had.

Carlos followed his gaze. He eyed JP's bag. "What's in there?"

"Nothing!"

"I thought I saw something move in the coffee shop just a moment ago, Toby's coffee shop."

"Look—"

But the normally timid Carlos cut him off. "Do you know what will happen if he finds out? He'll probably break your other leg. What could be so worth it?"

Speechless, JP felt the weight of the objects in his bag. But why would Carlos stand up to him and not Toby? Toby had practically tortured him, and JP had never done anything to him. Well, maybe he had found out about the jars. But it still didn't make sense, or at least, not to JP.

"Look, you're not my mom. I don't have to listen to you. And I don't owe you anything."

"Me? What does this have to do with me? It's you this will harm."

The look of incredulity on Carlos's face only made JP

mad. Carlos thought he was stupid, didn't he? It's why he had been so shocked when he brought up Aquinas. Carlos was acting like JP's parents, or any one of his teachers.

"Yeah. It's about me. So let me make my own choices and face my own consequences without being nagged."

Carlos was left there, jaw hanging open in disbelief. But who cared? JP finally had his prize, and there was no way Toby would even find out.

When JP hobbled up to his room, he sighed and took off his backpack. He lay down on his bed width wise and stared at the ceiling. What an experience. Such terror, such joy. It was worth stealing the bottle just to have felt this strange and incredible way.

JP woke the next morning to the burning of his leg from the stress he put it through the night before. The tequila was too special. It deserved more ceremony than he could muster after such a night, and he had an unshakable feeling that he should share it with Jessica, so he selected his remedy in the form of the Weller Antique 107. It was finer stuff than he was used to, but a shot of it did the trick, and then another for good measure.

The sun shone in through his half-parted curtains. It really felt like a new day for JP. It was more than just the knowledge that the sun had risen but the feeling of sunshine on his shoulders and the warmth of a September day and of the fine bourbon in his stomach. He had no plans, but it seemed wrong to even suggest planning on a day that felt so right. How could planning make it any better?

Maybe he'd do something simple, find a nice spot on the roof, soak up some rays while reading that book he'd started. Strange how he resented that reading was the only thing he could do the past couple weeks but now, with a little attitude shift, it was a pleasure. The tequila and bourbon were already out of the pack and hidden under his bed, but when he reached into the pink bag for the book, he only pulled out the T-shirts he wrapped the bottles in. Confused, he unzipped the side pocket. There was nothing there but a piece of paper titled "Appointment Confirmation." But where was the book? He knew exactly where it was when he heard yelling. The shouts were, of course, from Toby.

Stuffing the piece of paper in his pants pocket, JP went up to the window and hid himself behind the curtain as he peeked down. The chubby man was red-faced, steaming, and crossing the street. Wooden baseball bat in one hand and a small paperback book in the other. But his approach was all wrong. He wasn't heading to the butcher shop, but to Carlos's bookstore. JP saw Carlos come out and could also see what happened when Toby reached him.

JP's eyes burned as he watched. The entire world disappeared, vanished, all of it except the sight of Toby and Carlos. Poor, poor Carlos. Poor, poor Carlos. Once and then twice and then again and again. JP's hand rubbed his eyes but came away dry. Why were they so dry?

JP didn't notice when Toby left, because it continued to play in his mind. Over and over again. When he realized it was only in his head, he silently, softly, weakly made his way down to the street. Jessica was nowhere to be seen.

But Carlos —

4

JP's crutch brushed something on the pavement. The book. Half open, with a sprinkling of red dots disfiguring its pages. The book JP had left at the coffee shop.

He stared blankly down at the red-peppered pages. He hated this book. He despised it all the more because in hating it, he found a reason not to raise his eyes. Not to look at Carlos. But he could not maintain this delusion for long. His gaze crept up to look at the man. Or what was left of him. Carlos's face was blank, and unharmed. His arms, too, were untouched. So too his chest and stomach. But his legs—they had been beaten into a fine jelly from the rhythmic swing of Toby's bat.

It looked like the raspberry jelly Carlos had cherished so much. The raspberry jelly JP had smashed.

Carlos had fainted after the first few strikes, but Toby had continued. If Toby had intended to simply punish Carlos, he would have wanted him to be awake. Instead, he chose to maim him. Chose to take his legs. If Carlos survived, he could never escape Toby. He could not run away. His life would be a never-ending torture.

If Carlos survived.

Words dripped out of JP's mouth. They were so quiet and weak that JP barely realized he was speaking. "I— I thought— it was supposed to be me. This was not what I wanted. I just— it was a stupid bottle—"

The words started to flow out, faster, almost clogging up his tongue, but down on the ground, Carlos remained still. The unconscious figure would hear none of JP's explanations, none of his justifications, how he never thought it would happen like this, and it was just over a few bottles of alcohol, and he needed that tequila to remind him and, and, and—

Every word of it, fell on deaf ears. Every word of it was hollow. JP had only one real answer, he had wanted to do what he wanted to do, and he had not cared about the consequences because his life, the life he chose outweighed them. But here, the consequences affected Carlos.

JP thought they would only be his. But the sight of Carlos's legs, or rather, lack of legs, made him question whether any choice only affected the person who made it. After all, he was a part of the world, and anything that affected him affected the world he was a part of.

What strength JP had, failed him. The crutches fell from his grasp, and he sank to his knees, not noticing the pain in his leg. Carlos's face was still as stone, but in JP's imagination, it was telling a story. "I tried to warn you. Tried to help," it said, "but you would not listen, and now my blood is on your hands."

JP had to do something, anything, to right this wrong, but everything that came to mind was either not enough or wrong in itself. To avenge Carlos would be pointless, and Carlos would despise JP all the more for it. It would double his suffering. As it was, JP thought that a life of such suffering was not worth living.

"Then that's what I can do for you," JP said, voice trembling, "that's what I can do. I can end it."

Parked a few yards away was the white SUV he had driven into town, Madison's white SUV. Grabbing his crutches, JP climbed to his feet. He hobbled over, mind solely focused on getting to the car, almost forgetting his purpose other than to get there.

He got in. The key sat on the front seat where he had left it. What a stroke of fortune that he left it there. Almost like it was his fate, his destiny, his doom, to be here in this car. The engine roared, and the lights of the dashboard flicked on. He put the stick in reverse and checked his mirror. A muttered, "I'm sorry," slipped through his lips, and the car sped back, right over Carlos's head.

For a second, JP lingered there, wondering why he was rubbing his eyes when there were no tears coming. He gripped the steering wheel till his hands turned white. It stopped his fingers from shaking, but the spasms spread down to his arms.

I need a cigarette. I need a cigarette. That's it. My fingers won't stay still because I need a cigarette.

JP was half convinced of it. But he needed to get out of here. Out of this spot. Out of this town. It was too bright. Too bright. And he needed a cigarette. He needed to go find one. That's why he needed to get out of here.

JP put Madison's car into drive and sped off while wondering why he could not simply go to the room above the butcher shop and grab one of the packs he had there.

The roads were barren. Old trucks lay in ditches, covered in branches and the new growths of vines. Deer peeked their heads out from the foliage that lined the road to see the strange thing speeding down their way. They had already forgotten that these noisy machines once filled these streets, day and night. The world had already moved on. It no longer thought of the humans who once ruled it. But JP believed that everything now thought of him and the deed he had done.

Every curious squirrel, every low-hanging branch was trying to catch him, stop him, punish him! He was half tempted to stop and let them. But he could not lift his good foot from the gas. Every ray of sunlight that reflected in his rearview mirror increased his anxiety. They were after him. *They.* Not Toby. What would Toby care? Though maybe he would be mad about losing his victim and might imagine JP would make a good replacement.

But Toby was not chasing him.

Nor was Jessica. She might not care either, or she might despise him, but she would not give chase. There was no law to pursue him. No. But he was fleeing. He was running from himself, from the whole world. One of these two were guilty, maybe both. But as the car tore down the country lane, JP remembered that the world had vanished. That left only him.

Some might think he was obviously the guilty one, but it was not obvious to JP. Knowing what brought him to it, when he really did it, he had already justified it in his mind and his heart. JP thought it would be just, to relieve Carlos of his suffering, a suffering JP was partially responsible for. But his heart now rebelled. Somehow, his heart and desire had convinced him to steal the bottle against what he knew was right, but now his mind had convinced him of the justice of a great evil his heart could not stand. His heart would either repent or die.

He did not choose either option right then. He had stopped the car. Through the windshield, he viewed the white farmhouse with the solar panels. The one he had stayed in those first few days. They were a dream to him, those days, although they were dreams back then too, seen through a haze of alcohol. He turned off the car and waited. But neither pursuer was ready to strike him yet. The world and its laws were gone. He was free of them. But this, this was not freedom. He had always imagined being free from his parents and his teachers. There would be no one to punish him. But they were gone, and yet he felt condemned. Maybe he had never known what freedom was.

Wasn't he free before? After all, despite his parents and teachers and the law, he had done whatever he wanted. Maybe it was not freedom he desired, but simply to escape the consequences of it. The world had gone, but the consequences remained. In fact, they were worse now than before. What he would give to be grounded, to sulk in his room, cursing the injustice of his parents, opposed to sitting in this car. Madison's car.

Old guilt sprang up at the thought of her name. How could he have ever made those mistakes? Yes, he had been drunk, but why would he get drunk if he knew it might lead to hurting her? He never wanted to see anything but that awkward smile on her face. He knew if she was aware of just a portion of the things he'd done, he would have never seen it again. Now, he never would anyway.

JP remembered the piece of paper he found in her bag. He reached into his pocket and unfolded it. It was a printed email. A confirmation for an appointment with an obstetrician. It took him a moment to realize what that meant. A pregnancy doctor.

JP recalled the squirrel. He recalled what he thought of that pregnancy test at the time, how lucky that girl was to dodge the burden.

The paper fell through his shaking fingers. Madison had been—

The car door opened, and JP stumbled out. The porch steps were steep, much steeper than they were when he was there before. They grew taller as he approached. He crawled up them. His crutches were lost, left somewhere in the blur of this last hour. Everything, everything had changed. He was no longer pursued only for the actions of that day but for all the things that he had done. Even the house had changed. A few of the bullet holes he left had been patched. Someone was living here. Someone who had made an effort to mend the damages he caused. Maybe they could mend him. If only souls could be mended like damaged walls with a little bit of plaster.

The wood echoed as his knuckles knocked on the door. He leaned against the doorway and softly tapped. All the strength he could muster filled those quiet raps. Maybe no one would hear him. He would surely die on this porch, lacking the desire to live. He lacked any desire. All that was left were two vacant holes. One for Carlos and one for Madison and their—

A face appeared in the window of the door. A girl, maybe a little older than him. She wore a frown. Mild surprise, worry maybe. JP couldn't read her expression because all he could see was his own misery reflected in the glass.

"What can I do for you?" she asked politely, her voice muffled through the door.

"I need help." His voice was empty. He barely had enough breath to make it heard through the thick wood. Her gaze considered him for a long moment. The lock turned, and she opened the door. She looked him up and down till her eyes focused on his leg.

"You're bleeding!" She came over and supported him so he could take the pressure from his injured leg. Funny, he hadn't even noticed the wound had reopened. They went into the living room, and she helped JP into an armchair.

"Here, lift your leg on this," she said, pulling over the coffee table. "I think I have some gauze in the bathroom. I'll be right back."

She rushed out of the room and made a racket sifting through drawers and shelves. When she came back, JP hadn't moved. He didn't do anything but stare, stare at the bullet holes that littered the drywall. She sat on the ground right next to the coffee table.

"Oh my," she said as she peeled off the blood-soaked bandages. She looked up at his face and asked, "What's your name?"

"John," he said, without any consideration to why he used his given name.

"My name's Maria." She grabbed a white towel and a bottle of antibiotic cream or something and started to clean the wound. He didn't even wince when she applied the medicine.

"How did this happen?"

"A car accident," JP said without hesitation or thought. She furrowed her brow in doubt but continued.

"Oh. Well, you're pretty lucky if this was your only injury."

"Yeah, I'm the lucky one."

She started to rewrap the wound slowly and precisely. "What does that mean?"

"Someone else wasn't so lucky. Someone got hurt—got killed, killed by me."

She tied the wrapping off and then looked up at him with large, reflective blue eyes. But JP was still staring at the bullet holes. He opened his mouth slowly and said, "The worst part of it is that it happened all for a stupid desire of mine."

She got up and sat Indian-style on the couch beside the armchair. "What was that desire?"

"Tequila," JP said.

"You were drunk?"

"Yeah, I was drunk," he said to himself.

Maria frowned.

"I was completely wasted." He looked right ahead. Looked right at Maria. But he was seeing inside of himself. "I didn't see anything wrong with it, either. It was how I thought life ought to be spent. Not thinking and worrying about consequences, focused solely on the moment, on what I wanted, when I wanted it. Who wouldn't? Everyone I ever knew did the same. Or maybe just those I liked. And many I didn't like. I thought it was unjust that those I hated got to do what they liked, and I didn't. So, when it came down to it, I just thought about me and the tequila I wanted. And no one else. Then I crashed, and he died."

Maria listened passively, with understanding, with sympathy, not with judgment, not with condemnation, not with any of the hate JP was listening to himself with.

"I forgot about him. I guess I was too focused on me. On my self-experience, my self-expression, my self-liberation. I didn't realize I was being selfish."

They were both silent for a while. Maria looked down at the floral carpet, a sad frown upon her face.

And JP stared off again at the bullet holes. He didn't expect her to comment. In fact, if she tried, if she had some word of comfort, he would have gotten up and left. He did not deserve comfort. He could not stand the idea that there might be healing for him. Even if there was hope.

Not finding what she was hoping for amongst the flowers on the rug, Maria followed his gaze. "I didn't make those. Someone shot up the place before I got here. I tried to patch them, but I'm not exactly a handyman."

JP grimaced. "I don't blame you. I've aways been better at making holes than fixing them, sometimes it just takes more than what you have to put something back together."

Maria's face fell. Maybe she realized he didn't really mean the holes in the wall.

"Would you like some tea?" she asked. "I was just about to make some for myself, and I have some chocolate wafers too."

She did not wait for a response. The kettle was whistling in a few minutes, and she came back with a whole tray filled with sugar, snacks, and tea.

JP had stopped looking at the bullet holes—maybe he considered them a lost cause. Instead, he held the one framed picture left intact in the house. It was a polaroid of this woman,

Maria, giving a big kiss to a smiling infant boy. In the background was a street with cars stopped in the middle of it, and farther back was the ash heap of a house that had burned down. This picture had been taken after *the Vanishing*.

But JP saw no sign of childcare around this house.

"Who is the boy?" JP asked as he accepted the cup of tea.

Maria looked down at the black surface of her own tea with a fond smile. "His name is Thomas. He is my little hero. That very first day, when everything happened . . ." Her smile flickered at the memory of all the things she lost but did not disappear entirely. "I was wandering around in a daze, trying to put my half-finished medical degree to use, pulling people out of fires, and then there he was. His parents had disappeared. He lay quietly in a stroller all alone. So, I took care of him." Her smile broadened as she fell deeper into remembrance.

"Where is he now?"

"I gave him to someone. I met a woman one day while looking for baby formula in a supermarket. She saw me with Thomas and peeled over, bawling her eyes out. She had a baby too, and then he disappeared, a little Simon. She asked only to hold Thomas, but I could see all she wanted to do was be a mom again. So, I asked her to stay with us and soon let her keep him."

"You seem awfully glad, for having given up that baby."

"He was never mine to begin with. I am just glad I could give him a mother and that mother a son."

JP wanted to move on from the subject. "Haven't you done anything new, had any fun experiences since everything disappeared, since there was nothing to keep you from anything you wanted?"

"Of course." Maria looked confused by the question. "I took care of a baby all on my own for a while. There's nothing more incredible than supplying life to those who would have lost it otherwise. I never thought I'd really get to have it in that way, a family, a child. I had chosen to give my life to becoming a doctor, but there is hardly any time to think of a family with that profession. But God blessed me in a way I could never have expected, at a time I could not have looked for blessings."

"What's so good about it?" JP whispered. Maria looked up from her cup. But he stared at her with wide, pleading eyes. She smiled once again at her tea. "Have you never held a little baby in your arms? Felt his pulse against your chest? Had his fingers wrapped around yours? Then, he opens his eyes and sees you, and he smiles like you're all his world. And then when he cries, he cries out for you, because you're the only one he trusts to understand him. He's wonderful, beautiful, and despite all the difficulty that came with it, I only remember these moments."

"And you gave him up?"

"I knew how special he made me feel, and I knew what that woman had lost. Her Michael had been torn away from her. There is no sorrow to compare with that. And I know where they are and will be meeting them soon. They'll never lose their place in my heart." Maria looked up to JP from her sweet remembrance, and her face fell to confusion from the stream of tears flooding down his cheeks.

Maria said nothing.

JP didn't stop crying.

She adjusted herself on the couch and brushed her hair out of her face. Her cup was finally cool enough to drink, so she busied herself with the tea.

JP didn't notice her; he was too busy weeping. Then it struck him that this was always how he acted, so wrapped up in himself that he couldn't see that there was another person right next to him. Now might be the only time he was justified in it, but she must feel confused and uncomfortable. He stopped crying, at least on the outside.

"Do you have any whiskey to put in here?" he asked, despising himself as he said it. But it was all too late now anyway.

"No, I don't, and you probably shouldn't be drinking with an injury like that."

"Well, you are the doctor, I guess." His lips rose slightly as he gazed at his own cup. Blowing on the hot surface, JP took a sip. A tired sigh escaped him after he tasted the flavor of the tea. "Raspberries," he said. "Yep, I deserve it, don't I?"

They did not talk much after that. The sun rose higher and then began to sink.

Maria had done a good job with his bandages, but JP did not notice his leg. She tried to take care of him the best she could, always asking if he needed anything. She even helped him over to the bathroom and then back to the chair.

"Is there anyone I can bring you to, or would you like to stay here? I can bring down some pillows and sheets for the couch."

In answer, JP stood up. When she began to tell him how his leg needed to remain still, he cut her off. "So you believe in God?"

"Yes."

"I don't. Could you pray for me to Him?"

"I will."

"Thank you."

He walked toward the front door, not caring about the contradiction of his request, not caring about the consequence for his leg. And despite her continued pleas to stay and rest, he opened the door and said, "Thank you, again. I wish—I wish we could have met before all this. You seem like a good person. You seem like you care. I've known both kinds of people. But I guess I never thought you could be both. But I gotta go now.

I gotta go. You can't hold me. You can't catch me. Not now. Not after the crash. Not me."

Her eyes were big with a plea, a plea to stay, or maybe it was just pity. She watched him leave and then called out, "I'll pray for you."

On the road again, he drove the way he had come. He pulled up behind the butcher shop and retrieved the tequila and a pack of cigarettes from his room. He made the short walk to Carlos's bookshop and climbed the ladder attached to the back of the building. His leg felt like fire. It had hardly hurt since the morning. Even when Maria was wrapping it, JP felt nothing. Nothing from his body. He went over to the edge that overlooked Main Street and sat down, feet dangling in the open air.

JP gazed down at the corpse of the man he had murdered. None of his other companions were in sight. Two cars were missing from the street. They were gone, unable to face the body. He didn't blame them. Well, maybe he blamed Toby. Did Toby regret what he did? Did he hate JP for finishing him off?

Taking a cigarette from the pack, he lit it. But his lips were trembling, so it fell from his mouth and over the edge. He took out another. But his fingers were shaking too badly for him to light this one. It fell too. Again, he tried and tried. When the pack was empty, he tossed it too, over the edge.

JP uncorked the tequila but could not lift it to his lips. He looked down at the brown bottle with the blue label mournfully. His arm went limp, and the liquid trickled down to the street below.

"I wish I had been like her, like Maria," he said to himself. "She took care of that baby with evident joy; she gave him up with evident joy. She helped me, a stranger, a murderer, when I deserved nothing but pain."

If only. If only.

JP would never know the feeling of his own baby's pulse upon his chest. He would never know those tiny fingers wrapped around his, the smile, the tears, the love.

He would never know.

He had never thought that he could share such a joy with Madison. He would have only thought of it as a burden. Burden. Now, he wished she had burdened him. Burdened him with love. Burdened him with joy. Burdened him with their child.

JP looked out at the world, or rather, where the world used to be. He was mournfully glad it had vanished. He was glad because he knew what he would have done when Madison told him. He would have rejected her. He would have rejected their baby. He never thought that his actions would affect anyone but him and maybe the intended recipient. He never thought Carlos would get hurt. He never thought he'd bring another life into being.

But now that he knew, knew all that he had done, he could not bear it. If the world were still there, it might have caught him in this despair. He might have been able to go on. Go on being selfish.

The cold setting sun streamed pillars of light through the distant trees as it sank down to meet the horizon. Clouds, dark and wet, were coming in from the North. The leaves were starting to change to gold and red.

JP shivered. A breeze blew away the last of the summer warmth. There would be gray clouds and rain from now on.

How do people last? How do they endure the cold, dark days for months until summer comes again? Where do they find the heat to keep from freezing?

Maybe it is just me who cannot endure. Maybe I am cold-blooded.

He looked up and down the street where the world ought to have been and yelled out to it, "Catch me!"

But the world had vanished, and there was no one there to catch John Philip Sheen.

ABOUT THE AUTHOR

Timothy Raddell was born in 2000 and discovered his desire to write during college in between his brief studies of philosophy and classical languages. Abandoning these studies, he threw himself entirely into learning the craft of story. He founded his own publishing company to not only publish his own works but provide a medium for likeminded authors. He is from Cleveland, Ohio where he enjoys sailing with his father.

ABOUT THE TYPE

This book was set in Minion Pro, an Adobe Original typeface designed by Robert Slimbach. The first version of Minion was released in 1990. Minion Pro is inspired by classical, old-style typefaces of the late Renaissance, a period of elegant, beautiful, and highly readable type designs. Minion Pro combines the aesthetic and functional qualities that make text type highly readable with the versatility of digital technology.

CHECK OUT RADDELL PUBLISHING

Visit raddellpublishing.com for information on current and future publications, including more from Timothy Raddell.

CONTACT US

Email Us: tim@raddellpublishing.com

Find us on Facebook:
Facebook.com/RaddellPublishing

9 781962 105002